BLACK
SHUCK
BOOKS
Nov., 2025.

Visit Sunny
WHITSTABLE

The Confirmed Bachelors

The Confirmed Bachelors

by

Stephen Volk

For the two Steves, Gallagher and Laws

Contents

Ghosthunters I Have Known

a preface
by Stephen Volk

"Mallory: But you are a ghost hunter as well as an author?

Florence: Not really. You can't hunt what doesn't exist.

Mallory: Well that's just it. We think we have one which does."

The Awakening (2011)

"Mrs Moran, we want to believe you. We want to believe you very much."

The Entity (1982)

"Did it ever occur to you that this is the most interesting thing that's happened to you in your entire fucking life?"

Presence (2024)

I have met quite a few researchers and investigators of weird shit over the years, and have found them to be (variously) sensitive, chummy, thoughtful, boring, brainy, nice, snobby, dogmatic, self-important, and borderline deranged. One of the more pleasant elder statesmen of the tribe, the highly-esteemed Arthur Ellison, author of *The Reality of the Paranormal*, once told me if I gave him ten minutes he could prove to me that the nearby table did not, in fact, exist. Ciarán O'Keefe (resident sceptic on *Most Haunted*, now resident sceptic on Danny Robins' *Uncanny*) once introduced me to the crown prince of debunkers, James "The Amazing" Randi, who bent a spoon for me *à la* Uri Geller. And I've even talked to *The Science of Weird Shit* author Chris French himself and his "anomalous psychology" students at Goldsmiths college.

But my longstanding fascination with psychical research (which, as we know, Noël Coward exquisitely rhymed with the stately homes of England being "in the lurch") began with the entry drug of fiction.

For starters, I was shocked and transported when Arthur Conan Doyle used his booming, bearded hero from *The Lost World*, Professor Challenger, to investigate the world of Spiritualism in *The Land of Mist* only to have his blustery disbelief upended. Algernon Blackwood's John Silence stories intrigued and absorbed me when they cropped up regularly in horror anthologies in the sixties, in spite of being called by some his weakest stories, with speeches on esoteric topics "as silly as his name". An even sillier one belonged to William Hope Hodgson's pipe-smoking occult detective *Carnacki The Ghost Finder* whose cases alternated from having natural explanations to supernatural causes, such as the porcine thing in "The Hog" and a grotesque mouth in the floor of "The Whistling Room". To my delight, the ever-excellent Donald Pleasence played a cardigan-wearing Carnacki in *The Rivals of Sherlock Holmes* (1971) and, hokey or not, dated or not, it embedded in my psyche forever. "The

Horse of the Invisible" may be explained away at the end, Scooby-Doo fashion, but the disembodied sound of clacking hooves was the stuff of childhood nightmares.

I mustn't forget to mention also Dennis Wheatley's *Gunmen, Gallants and Ghosts* wherein I discovered his own character called "The Ghost Hunter", Neils Orsen, who he says was based on a man named Henry Dewhirst, a "great occultist" who foretold Wheatley would become a best-selling author. With titles like "The Case of the Thing That Whimpered" and "The Case of the Long Dead Lord", I was in.

True confession time.

The first TV series I ever wrote was called *Ghosthunter*. I was fifteen. The format involved two characters called Heller and Cavendish; one eccentric, the other straight. I can't say I wasn't influenced by *The Avengers* and *Department S*. It was an ITC series, in my head, in which the case-of-the-week was a supernatural one. I even designed the standing set, not a million miles from Steed's mews flat with pop art accoutrements. I imagined it starring Anton Rodgers and Michael Latimer. Even had a guest role for Fulton Mackay as a grizzled naysayer. And why not?

Since I knew no better, I had my duo as "agents" of the Society of Psychical Research, formed in 1882 by Sir William Barrett, Henry Sidgwick and Frederic Myers, hirsute academics intent on giving telepathy, crisis apparitions, spirit communication, and séances proper study. Not before time, you might say. At a time before Freud, let alone Richard Dawkins. A new spin was put on all this in 1962 when Trevor Hall wrote *The Spiritualists: The Story of Florence Cook and William Crookes*, claiming the research was a fraudulent cover for a sexual relationship between scientific investigator and medium. This I learned from an episode of *Victorian Scandals* (1976) called "The Frontiers of Science" which starred Ronald Hines as Crookes and Twiggy as Florence Cook (and her spirit alter ego "Katie King"). This is when I first started to think that you could take the supernatural out of a story and what remained was even more interesting than if you left the supernatural in.

Whether sex belongs in a ghost story is for Monty James and Robert Aickman to debate in the great hereafter, but sex reared its ugly head again in a remarkable drama called "To Lay a Ghost" (1971) in the final series of *Out of the Unknown*. Peter Barkworth plays Dr Walter Phillimore in a Colin Wilson turtleneck, brought in to address a domestic haunting which, notoriously, dramatises the supposedly repressed desires of a rape victim. Hence the title. Yet Barkworth stayed with me. Ordinary. Slightly sleazy. As believable as anyone in *The Wednesday Play*.

Sexism abounds, too, in Nigel Kneale's seminal 1972 Christmas day ghost story *The Stone Tape*, where a bunch of techies, sequestered to their new research facility, find the building acts as a recording medium, preserving past events in its very fabric. Intent on the appliance of science, Michael Bryant is gruff and obnoxious as Brock. Jane Asher looks on while the boys play with their toys, but I loved it.

Then there were the movies.

In Robert Wise's *The Haunting* (1963) based on the Shirley Jackson classic, English thespian Richard Johnson is Dr John Markway, head of a ghostbusting team making themselves cheerily at home inside a gothic cathedral of dread (notwithstanding that Nelson Gidding, who adapted the novel, considered it all set in an insane asylum, slamming doors and all).

The Legend of Hell House (1973), another of my favourites, duplicated the exact same format of a family unit (father, wife, stroppy teenagers) while gender-swapping the psychic into a camp Roddy McDowall, though character actor Clive Revill makes a damp squib of Dr Lionel Barrett (no doubt a knowing reference by writer Richard Matheson to the historical William).

I was expecting a derivative potboiler from 1982's *The Entity* but found it genuinely creepy and disturbing, more like *Alice Doesn't Live Here Anymore* than *The Omen*. As in the true case upon which it's based, university doctors with their gizmos and eagerness enter the story of a woman sexually attacked by an invisible assailant. You might think they resemble Simon and Garfunkel, but in fact they're the spitting image of Russell Targ and Harold Puthoff, researchers into remote viewing (a form of clairvoyance) at Stanford Research Institute. Their motives are dubious. The male gaze evident. Finally they reduce Carla to a lab rat in a cage. But the film took its dirty subject seriously, blurring the boundary between parapsychology and psychology and that's how I like it.

James Herbert was still big in the eighties and it was only a matter of time before he created an investigator, which he did in the form of David Ash (played by Aidan Quinn in the film of *Haunted*, which I'd laboured on being a part of when it was in development as an ill-fated BBC TV series).

By the time I wrote *Ghostwatch* I wanted my own parapsychologist, Dr Lyn Pascoe, to be convincing and real, so I talked to women in the field: Serena Roney-Dougal, whom I first saw riding a rainbow-decorated bicycle in Glastonbury; Susan Blackmore, one of the first scientists to theorise oxygen starvation as the explanation behind near death experiences. I also enlisted Guy Lyon Playfair, who'd investigated the Enfield poltergeist with Maurice Grosse, to come in and talk to the cast about what it was like to be in a real-life haunted house.

Of course the "onion skin" of the past, peeled away to reveal older, darker forces is straight out of Kneale's *Stone Tape* playbook. In my mind, at least, Quatermass, his scientist-hero, was something of a parapsychologist too, by default. The rational mind battling the apparitional (even telekinetic) forces in *Quatermass and the Pit* indivisible in my mind from Brock in *The Stone Tape* or Dr Markway in *The Haunting*.

Afterlife (2005-6) was about a medium, but my Dr Robert Bridge (Andrew Lincoln), though a sceptic, wasn't a ghosthunter, more like a modern equivalent of M.R. James's university-based scholars, bookish, solitary and emotionally impaired. It's worth noting that Jonathan Miller's *Whistle and I'll Come to You* (1968) omits a scene that begins the original short story of 1904 in which Parkins' friend offers to share the double-bedroom and be "company for you" – a suggestion the Professor rejects, saying it would "hinder his work". This omission, some might say, diminishes the climax of its irony when someone – or some *thing* – *does* share the room. Mark Gatiss called a spade a spade when he said Parkins (who MRJ describes as "something of an old woman") is clearly a closeted gay man – basically James himself – whose fear of hairy things and crumpled bedlinen inevitably takes on a new dimension.

Mainstream British television returned to the world of psychical research after a long famine with ITV's tentative pilot *Harry Price Ghost Hunter* (2015) based on Neil Spring's novel and highly fictionalized character, badly miscast in the form of Rafe Spall. Jonathan Rigby did a much better job of portraying the real Price in the inventive *Borley Rectory* (2017) directed by Ashley Thorpe, while Spall Sr. (Timothy) had better luck playing the part of Maurice Grosse in the effective but occasionally over-wrought chiller *The Enfield Haunting* for Sky. (I'd been asked to adapt it, but declined. Been there, done that.)

Full disclosure. Some writers love the tropes of the gangster film. Others, the conventions of the whodunit. I'm addicted to the paraphernalia of the ghosthunting trade. Scenes of crackly phonograph recordings from beyond the grave, or, as in *The Awakening* (2011), photographs set off by tripwires – many of such tropes, I now realise, plucked unconsciously from my memory of "The Horse of the Invisible".

When I met Rebecca Hall on set, she told me she started reading the script and thought, "Ah, I see. By the end she's going to believe in ghosts." A thinly-veiled criticism, but I thought: "Yes! That's exactly what I want the audience to anticipate. That's the journey we are on." For me, scoffing is what fans the flames of expectation. Plus it's fun to write. Always.

Florence Cathcart was essentially a synthesis of Robert and Alison, my two characters from *Afterlife*. The surface rationalist who wants to put everything in a box, and the trauma victim who knows reality is not what it seems. She has to confront that undesirable truth and survive it, if she can; that's the implicit promise. That's the sceptic's journey, be it *Afterlife* or Dana Andrews in *Night of the Demon*.

The obvious reason I'm attracted to these types of characters is that the rational versus irrational is a delicious battle of opposites. My first exposure to which was probably Sherlock Holmes applying his big brain to the seemingly preternatural *Hound of the Baskervilles*.

More than that, I love the core absurdity, madness, and sheer theatricality of using science and technology to address the metaphysical. *Ghostwatch*, for instance, ridiculously, uses the tools of light entertainment to try to answer the most profound question of human existence; do we survive death? For me, that contradiction says much about who we are as a species – frightened, logical, driven, grasping, failing, indefatigable, and full of an incredible capacity for belief.

Thirdly, these characters embody in a powerful way one thing I think might be essential in a ghost story. Doubt. To me, if someone accepts the supernatural, we might have something else very good, we might have *Blithe Spirit* or *Randall and Hopkirk (Deceased)*, but for a ghost story I believe we need "the engine of doubt".

As you'll see in the stories that follow.

"The Confirmed Bachelors" is a new one. Steve Shaw has been kind enough to publish it herewith, and suggested, since it's (on the surface at least) about a ghost, we might team it up with another ghost story of mine, "The Waiting Room". The latter is based on a true story. So, actually, is the former. The facts will be easy to find for those with an enquiring mind, but I'm not going to give the game away here.

I leave it to you to investigate the unknown at your leisure. And remember those who took steps into the dark before you. With an upturned wine glass or an EMF meter. Donald Pleasence or Dr Pascoe.

But don't expect ghosts, necessarily.

There's no such thing, you know…

The Waiting Room

O UR hosts, such as they were, did not seem as subject to the cold as we did, remaining cheerful beyond requirement as they furnished us with cups of tea. We had not divulged the exact purpose for our coming, though one of them at least had experienced the phenomenon, and I could only reason that their lightness of spirit was born of the knowledge that they would soon be off to a warm bed, and we would not.

"*Au revoir.*"

"He means goodbye. Does he mean goodbye?"

"He does, my dear," said the station master. "Until the morrow morn."

The man and his doughty wife having departed, we were alone, and my companion turned down the wick of the signal man's lamp, saving it, I presumed, lest when the darkness came, we should be more needful of it. He placed a travel clock upon the table between us, assuring me that the instrument kept good time, adding the *caveat* that such instruments were prone to be affected by such – he paused… *atmosphere* as we were there to witness.

"What shall we do?" We sat with blankets over our knees and scarves wrapped around our necks, and had not yet divested ourselves of hats.

"We shall wait," said Dickens, laying down his note book and pencil beside our scant means of illumination. "This is a waiting room. We shall wait."

* * *

THE first time I set eyes on him in the flesh it was with his back to me, frock coat splayed, hair salted by the limelight, proclaiming to the balcony with a theatricality befitting a Hamlet, though the words were not those of the Bard of Avon but his own. Even then, I strangely felt I already knew him, such was his fame, and such was the intimate vividness of his works. I was not alone. When an actor takes to the stage, he invariably wants the audience to love him. The extraordinary thing was, with Dickens, it was the other way around; the audience wanted *him* to love *them*.

The performance, as expected, was intoxicating. Each character sprang alive not just from his lips but from every inch of his physical being. At times, his voice boomed like a Wesleyan; at others, softened so gently as to make the audience lean forward as one. He tickled the belly of the trout like a master, and if he were any normal man I'd have wagered it would take it out of him, but he seemed forever lifted by the rapt attention of the crowd. Two thousand strong they were, that night. His adoring public, out in force, and I almost regretted I was not there to applaud him to high heaven.

Far from it.

While his words flowed like a river my own throat was dry with fear. It had taken some Dutch courage to get me to the wings, and I hoped he would not smell it on my breath.

Steel was required to confront a treasure the equal of the Crown Jewels who no doubt thought himself impregnable. I had something to tell the most beloved writer in England, and I was by no means sure how he would take it.

The ghost story drew them in as it came to a close. The resolution was upon us. I knew every word – and not because I had read it in *All the Year Round*. I told myself, not for the first time, to curb any anger I felt rising. The opponents were not well matched and the one who would suffer, ultimately, if I let loose, would be me.

The final line was delivered with a flourish. Dickens' hand rolled in a wave from his breast and his fingers unpeeled from his fist as the last three words were spoken in a whisper. I saw, from behind, the merest twitch of a smile in the corner of his mouth. The house erupted, jumping to their feet, stamping for more. I marvelled at the suppleness of his spine as he took bow after extravagant bow. Three steps to the edge of the stage, three steps back. Then he strode to the wings, his visage leaving the light.

Inches away from me, he tore off his cravat and knocked back a glass of sherry with a raw egg beaten into it, which was lying in wait on a silver tray proffered by a stagehand.

"Sir—"

The ghost story drew them in as it came to a close.

"At the door! At the door!"

"My name is Thomas Frank Heaphy," I said.

"Very likely. Very likely."

Cuffs askew, he returned to the standing ovation, lapping it up, delivering a swift, sentimental homily to send his public home with a warm heart – and the name of his next volume deftly placed in their ears. I was only glad we had been spared the death of Little Nell.

A glass of rum with cream awaited after his second curtain call, and a glass of champagne followed the third. The uproar gradually abated. The reading was over. He left the stage for the last time.

"Mr Dickens, sir—" I watched him walk past me. "The story, sir. 'The Portrait Painter's Story'…" He stopped then, and turned back. I think because he was expecting a compliment on his writing, his performance, or both. I gave him neither. I gave him this: "The story is mine, sir."

"What?"

"The story you told. The story you *printed*. It happened to me."

A snarling laugh exploded from lips shiny with rum. "You are mad!"

"Would that I were."

"Would that you *were*? You *are*! There is no concept more certain! Now be off with you, and take such nonsense to the street." The dark of backstage and the darkness of the author became one. No limelight to lift the make-up on his cheeks now as he pawed away flowers from well-wishers. Nothing to disguise the furrowed brow. His rage, diluted only by an innate sense of gentlemanly decorum, resulting in – dismissal. But I was not about to be dismissed.

"I am that portrait painter."

"You are a fool, sir."

"I am not. I have no wish to give you discomfort, but you must hear me out. I shall not leave until you do."

"We shall see about that." Dickens grabbed the arm of someone in a suit I took to be the stage manager. "This man is—"

"Please! Just listen. The story happened to me. Precisely as you told it. I know it sounds preposterous. It—"

"Sir, a ghost story *cannot* be true because ghosts are *not* true. That much is quite *surely* preposterous. Now please! Leave me in peace and be on your way without further disturbance. Or I fear I shall have to – George! By all the saints in—"

"But I have *proof*," I barked, not waiting for his reply, and, lifting my voice as he showed me his back, stuck my dagger in: "Your story appeared in September, did it not? Well, by then I had already sent the manuscript of my experience to a different magazine. A rival of yours, as it happens. The editors can verify the exact date of its arrival. It is planned to appear in the Christmas issue."

Dickens went very cold very quickly, and dismissed the stage manager summarily with a fluttering gesture, after which he deigned to step closer to me, as if to keep our dialogue away from prying ears.

"Are you threatening me, young man?"

"No."

"Are you asserting foul play? That by some unknown and unbelievable method, your story fell into my hands?"

"I am only asserting," I said boldly, "what I know to be true. I was your protagonist."

"No! You are my antagonist! That much is plain!"

"Then read it and see for yourself. Here is a run of the proof pages." I thrust against his chest a sheaf of paper I had been carrying under my arm. Dickens recoiled no less sharply than if I had drawn a pistol.

"I shall do no such thing! I shall see my lawyer and you would do well to see yours."

He spun away. It took no great observational skill to see anger and discombobulation under the bluster. Anger that his integrity was being questioned. The *originality* of his *ideas* questioned. The very lifeblood of his creativity – his *soul*. How could he have responded otherwise?

"Sir, this need not involve lawyers. Please hear me out. I am no more able to explain—" Burly figures tried to hold me back. "Mr Dickens! I can only think some supernatural agency is at work."

"I can only think you are talking utter poppycock!"

"You explain it then!" I broke away from my captors and grabbed him forcibly by one shoulder, spinning him around to face me and thrusting my manuscript firmly into his hands.

"I have no desire to. Nor shall I!" said Dickens, dropping it into a fire bucket in his close proximity, from which I had the ignominious pleasure of extracting it as I watched the door of the dressing room slam closed after him, before being unceremoniously ejected from the premises.

No curtain call. No encore. And certainly no flowers.

* * *

I am a painter, and though I have had cause to doubt the evidence of my eyes, and many will doubt what follows, I stand by every word of it, and shall not waver in my vow that it is an account of absolute veracity.

One morning in May 1858, I was seated in my studio at my usual occupation when I received an unexpected visit from a friend whose acquaintance I had made a year or two previously in Richmond Barracks, Dublin. Beholden to greet him in the hospitable manner in which he had entertained me when our roles had been reversed, I immediately offered him refreshments. Before either of us knew it, two o'clock saw us well ensconced in conversation, cigars, and a decanter of sherry. At that exact hour the bell rang. I found myself facing a well-dressed man and woman who asked for me by name. They could see I was entertaining, apologised for the intrusion, and said, in brief, that they wished, on recommendation, to commission me to paint their house in the country. Would I be free to do this in the coming autumn? I said indeed I would, and we parted, happily, with the gentleman leaving his card. Examining it later, however, I read the name JEREMIAH KIRKBECK – but no address. I subsequently tried to find evidence of the family in the Court Guide, with no success. So, frustrated, and not a little bewildered, I put the card in my writing desk and thought no more about it. It was an odd beginning to a tale that became significantly odder.

Come autumn, business took me to the north of England. It pained me to leave my wife and children even for a few nights, so when I alighted at York to paint a portrait of Lady Gertrude Delahunty it was with an inevitably heavy heart, especially as the dinner to which I was invited proved a far more substantial affair than I'd anticipated, and I was by no means a social animal. My host was already in his cups and his wife displayed considerably more of a bony chest in her low-cut Regency gown than I was prepared for. Children rattled up and down the staircase, by turns intrigued and scared, daring each other to see what the adults were up to, as if we were bogeymen. I should point out here that I have a defect in hearing which renders the effect of manifold voices as a dull, unintelligible blanket of sound, which causes me to adopt an expression of grinning stupor. However, through the din, suddenly I heard the name *"Kirkbeck"* – sharp as the cut of a knife. Compelled to interrupt the conversation I'd overheard, I asked if the family were resident in the neighbourhood, and was swiftly furnished with an address in Lincoln. Next morning I wrote to Mr Kirkbeck enquiring if the brief we had discussed in London was still open. A week later I received a letter in reply via the Post Office, York – which I had given as my return address – saying he was glad to hear from me and that, if it were agreeable, he would be delighted to accommodate my arrival the coming Saturday; furthermore, if it suited my plans, I could stay until Monday. I replied to confirm that such an arrangement would be perfect. My all too flattering portrait of the fearsome Lady Delahunty would be done by then, and I would be free.

The train from York to London was due to stop at Doncaster, then at Retford Junction, after which I would stay on the same line to Lincoln. The day was cold, wet, foggy and disagreeable – that of a typical English October. For the first part of the journey I was alone in the carriage, but at Doncaster a young woman got on. I was sitting next to the door with my back to the engine. Since this is known as the ladies' seat, I offered it to her, but she quietly declined and found the corner opposite.

I watched her settle and adjust herself, taking off her gloves, placing them on top of the rabbit-skin muff on her lap, and generally attending to matters of arrangement and plumage to which ladies are dedicated. Finally she lifted the veil from her hat to reveal a young person of perhaps no more than two- or three-and-twenty years, though if I removed her many matronly layers, perhaps two or three younger. Her hair was bright brown or auburn and I noticed she had delicately marked eyebrows, almost black. The warmth of the compartment had brought no blush to her cheeks, which remained as pale as marble, yet her expression had a depth and harmony about it that made her face, though not strictly regular, infinitely more attractive than mere perfection. Secreted in her corner, she showed what I took to be ill ease at being a lone woman in confined circumstances with a lone man. I saw no wedding ring. Nevertheless, wanting to be a gentleman rather than a boor, I found myself reluctant to inflict conversation upon a stranger who might not desire such a thing. To my surprise, it was she who initiated it.

Did I know what time the train passed through Retford? I said I wasn't sure, but I could consult my Bradshaw's, if she really wanted to know. She shook her head, thanking me almost inaudibly. Noticing the accoutrements of my trade on the luggage rack above my head, she asked what I did for a living. The smile the answer brought was soon replaced with unutterable sadness. It made me wonder if she had come from a funeral.

"Do you think you could paint my portrait?"

"Yes," I said. "I think I could, if I had the opportunity."

She looked at me, not in any peculiar or sinister fashion but one almost of simple but intense interest. "Do you think you could recall my features?"

"Yes," I laughed. "I am sure I shall never forget them."

She dropped her eyes slightly. "Of course, I might have expected you to say that; but do you think you could do me *from recollection alone?*"

This struck me as a bizarre request, almost a playful one, but I did my best to answer it. "Well, if it is necessary, I would try. But can't you give me any sittings?"

"No, it's impossible. It cannot be."

I laughed again, now thinking this a tease. "If you could grant me just one sitting, it would be better than none."

"No, I don't see that it could be."

I felt I had overstepped the mark and we both lapsed into silence. She stared out of the window at the countryside. I unfolded my newspaper. After three quarters of an hour we arrived at Retford, and she rose to get off.

"I daresay we shall meet again."

I could not, in all honestly, conceive of that eventuality, but said: "I hope we shall."

After she had departed, my thoughts strayed idly, and with some degree of shame, to a kiss I might have planted on that cold cheek, a different word spoken, a touch not made, a path not taken, to remorse and regret, if though a sweet one. The typography on the pages of *The Times* no longer held my interest and my mind wandered, returning to her strange, alluring and preposterous challenge – to remember her features. To draw her *from recollection.* Could I? *Would* I? I would.

Taking out a soft pencil and opening my sketch book, I would *try*, at least, while the freshness of our proximity still hung in the air, to catch that quality she had of a heron or swan. *Swan-like*, that was the word – not marble, but living and effortlessly graceful.

At the time I thought it no more than a way to pass the journey.

At half past five my travels ended and I disembarked in a dreary sleet at Lincoln. A pre-arranged landau drawn by a pair awaited me. Upon reaching the Kirkbeck residence, Lentney Hall, I was welcomed into a large conglomeration of family, friends, cousins, and servants, the details of which need not concern us, except to say that the gathering into which I was welcomed stood in stark contrast to the strange, quiet intimacy of my train journey.

I slept well. The business dealings were dealt with over the subsequent weekend, and I left on the Monday, pleased that my proposal as to the composition had been agreed and several preparatory drawings of the architectural detail undertaken. I am never more at ease than when concentrating on what I see and transferring that to paper. Consequently I found that the young lady in the railway compartment vanished from my thoughts almost completely.

Some weeks passed. Christmas was upon us. Eager to capture the wonder in the children's faces as they opened their presents, I opened my drawing pad accidentally to the page showing the sketch of the woman on the train, and to my surprise considered it not half bad. I'd caught her reticent posture. The arresting eyes. The layers of armour of her skirts and fur. "You should make a painting of her." My wife leaned over my shoulder. "No," I replied; "She must stay as she was, half-realised. Unfinished." I have no idea why I replied in such a way.

January saw another commission take me north once more, and on this occasion I had to switch at Retford Junction, but missed my connection. There was nothing for it, therefore, but to put up at the Swan Hotel for the night. I have a special dislike to passing an evening at a hotel in a country town. Dinner is invariably an indignity if not a punishment. Books are never to be had and local guides do not interest me. I had no inclination to learn more about the Venerable Bede, or the River Idle which once "ran foul with the blood of Englishmen". I ordered dry toast and tea, and whilst waiting for my order, it occurred to me how very peculiar it was that, on two occasions in the past six months, I had stopped at that very place. The words of my female travelling companion – her fervent belief that we would *meet again* – came as a peculiar frisson of memory. For no other reason than to dispel it, I took up my sketch book and began drawing the beer glass in front of me. The publican presently noticed my activity, and enquired if I did paid work. I answered that I did. He said a friend of his would give anything to have a painting of his daughter; it would mean the world to him. "Then I shall do it, gladly." He told me where the man lived – not many yards away, in Church Close, and asked if he could send him a note. I replied in the affirmative. The Publican left, then turned back to me. "Do not be alarmed by him. He is changed, but he is a good man." Before I could speak further, he had gone about his business.

Breakfast saw a reply begging me to postpone my current plans "as you would value the life and health of your own father". It was signed by one *Maria Lute*. Intrigued by such an entreaty, I immediately sent letters to rearrange my imminent appointments and arrived at the address, to be greeted by a fair to handsome girl of fifteen or so, clearly not a servant though she bade me sit by the fire and thrust a poker at the embers to revive it as if she were one. I asked what kind of portrait her father envisaged. She did not know. Watercolour or oil? And what size, as that is reflected in the price? She said only "My father wants the best." At that point a tall, stooped man came downstairs, took his coat from the hook, and left.

"Will he not be joining us?" I asked.

"Oh!" She emitted a small bleat of surprise and her back straightened in the chair. "That was the doctor. My father is indisposed."

I could see that I was not going to be terribly successful in extracting more information, so opened my sketch book and box of pencils. "Then shall we start? I can do a quick study. The pose just as you are is delightfully natural. The light from the window gives the quality of a Vermeer…"

Her face fell. Her mouth hung open, then she seemed to comprehend the misunderstanding at once, and with a shuddering intake of breath both laughed and seemed on the edge of tears.

"Mr Heaphy, the portrait is not to be of me. It is to be of my sister Caroline, who died four months ago. On September 13th, to be exact. My father was devotedly attached to her and, cruelly, has no record of her likeness." I quickly learned that it had been his one thought ever since the tragedy, and she hoped, if something of the kind could be done, it would improve his health, which was suffering abominably. Every day the pain of loss grew deeper and she feared that sooner or later he would sink beyond the doctor's reach. "He speaks only of wanting to end his life, so that he can be with her."

Sympathetic though I was, I was also perplexed. "But how can I draw a face I have never seen?"

"You must try."

Maria held back more tears, tilting her head towards her lap, and suddenly that sadness, that expression, made me think of another face I had encountered before.

"Miss Lute. Maria…" I was almost afraid to ask. "How did your sister die?"

I was told she had perished in a train crash, just outside the station at Retford Junction. I cannot describe sufficiently the hollow feeling I felt in the pit of my stomach, yet somehow I retained my capacities enough to show her the sketch in the front of my pad. The one I had made in the railway carriage back in October.

As she shot to her feet, I feared she would faint. I rose to grasp her by the elbow lest she did, but shortly her steadiness was assured and her gaze fixed on the drawing I held out in front of her.

"Let me take it to Papa."

Before long I heard a thin cry from upstairs. When she returned, Lute was on her arm, dishevelled, but glowing. How could this be? he asked. A minute's preparation had been enough for me to provide him a *half*-truth – that I had drawn his daughter months ago, by incredible coincidence, when we happened to be in the same train compartment. I did not say when. I did not say *after her death*. The words refused to come to my lips. Nor did I want them to. I was only happy that what I said placated their mystification.

A painting was commissioned. I executed it in London. Once it was completed, I returned north. Upon seeing it, father and daughter embraced each other tightly. "Uncanny," was the hushed verdict. They had no idea just how *uncanny* the true derivation of the artwork had been. Whilst I was applying the final lacquer, the spindly doctor came again to examine Simeon Lute, and pronounced his health remarkably, and permanently, restored. "Your arrival here was an act of God." How could I say it was not the act of God but the act of another that had guided me?

At the doorstep Maria declared it was all her father wanted; something to remember her by. "Caroline has given him that, through you."

I said: "It was what she wanted, also." But I said no more.

The portrait now hangs in his bedroom, with the following words engraved on a small frame plaque below it: *"C.L. - 13 September 1858, aged twenty-two."*

* * *

I returned home from St James's Hall, Piccadilly, feeling desolate, annoyed and foolish for not having anticipated Dickens' reaction. I suppose we hold our heroes in high esteem, so when they disappoint us as people, or treat us with contempt, the hurt is more than a blow one might feel from a mere stranger. But I was no idiot. I knew fame held the upper hand, and what was I? Nothing but a struggling nonentity. I had little hope of taking on the rich and powerful, even though I knew my tale was true. *Absolutely* true. Yet – how could it be? When it had come from Dickens' pen?

Waking with a thick head from wallowing in too many brandies the night before, I decided I had nothing to lose by taking the author's own caustic advice, and posted my manuscript to his business representative, John Forster.

Days passed. I received no reply. I expected to hear nothing, but the reality of doing so poured salt on the wound. To be dismissed was one thing, but to be *ignored?* Too distracted to work, I snapped at Eliza and the children, and the matter tortured me; not least the notion that I might be denied a solution to the confounded puzzle.

Then, one night, the bell rang. The gas lighting of the street gave my visitor's silhouette a halo which I might have rendered on canvas as a yellow line. In shadow, his face possessed an alarmingly grey pallor. My wife had opened the door wordlessly. When he saw the children clustered in night shirts at the foot of the stairs, he said: "I am Ebenezer Scrooge. I have come on the business of ghosts." He smiled broadly as he saw them run away giggling, but his eyes hardened to ice as he looked at me.

Without further introduction Dickens requested privacy. I took him to my studio while Eliza absented herself to the drawing room. I asked if I could take his coat. He did not answer.

"This strangeness. I appreciate…"

He cut me off. "You accuse me of plagiarism."

"That is far from my thoughts. I never said that."

Sitting down at my drawing board, he produced a leather-bound cheque book from his overcoat pocket and laid it flat. I saw the name of Messrs. Coutts & Compy, and his signature already made out with multiple underscores. My name was written in the space between *Pay to* and *or bearer* but the amount on the next line had not been filled in. He snatched a pen from a broken cup and dipped it in the ink pot next to it before looking up at me. "Well?"

I frowned.

"You have a price in mind."

"No."

"What do you make in a year?"

I was affronted. "A gentleman would never ask such a thing."

"I am not a gentleman," Dickens said tensely, rolling the pen in his fingers.

"I am not interested," I said. "Nor, I think, are you."

"You know nothing of me."

"I know what I see."

Which was a man who looked considerably older than his forty-nine years, whose visage was known to every household in the country. And if they could see him now, they would see what I did – a man afraid.

"Name your price. Please name your price and we shall have done."

"I will not, and you do me a disservice to think otherwise." I snatched the pen from his hand. "The only thing I want from you is the truth, so that I can pack this away in the dusty attic of my mind and forget about it. You think I enjoyed skulking around a theatre backstage waiting to pounce on you?"

"I have no idea what you enjoy. Human beings and their enjoyments are a continent of which exploration has revealed only a mere fraction."

"Very clever. Then let me put it like this. How do you think two stories written by perfect strangers can be identical?"

"They cannot."

"Do you think I must have read your mind? Read your thoughts before you had them? And then lied that those ideas were my own? The accusation, sir, is yours."

Bristling, Dickens walked away from me. Dickens prowled. Perhaps nobody had rounded on him quite like I had done. But I was at the end of my tether.

"I seek only an explanation," I said.

"And I do not?"

With his back to me he stared at an unfinished portrait of my wife. I could not tell whether he found it of merit or considered it ghastly. I saw only his clasped hands twitching at the small of his back.

He said he had talked to his lawyer and manager. I was uncertain whether he meant one man or two. He admitted he had been riled, horribly. "Inexcusably." Then *gave* an excuse – which was that similar slings and arrows had been outrageously flung in his direction before. "When you are young and published in piffling numbers, nobody says you stole their ideas. Oh no! But as soon as you are rich and reviewed and *fêted*, all manner of snakes crawl from under the rocks with their *Davy Copperheads* or *Olivia Twists!* You take so many to court you begin to wonder, head against your pillow, if you ever had a thought of your own in your entire life. Half the time they want to hang on your shirt tails, the other half you spend as Prometheus on the rock having your liver pecked out. Not a bad theme for a painting, if I may say so."

"It's been done," I said laconically. "Rubens, amongst others."

"I'm sure you could make it your own."

I wasn't sure if he was serious.

Dickens rested himself on the stool I kept for models, a weary lion resigned to lick his wounds. His coat over-spilled onto the paint-stained floorboards, looking like black wax from a night-long candle. Head downturned, his beard was hard to separate from his Elysian beaver collar. With his duck egg blue cravat loosely knotted he retained the semblance, under the air of respectability, of a dissolute fop.

It transpired his lawyer had examined both versions, and had found them "similar, *very* similar… very *extraordinary*…" – even down to the date, the very *date* I had used at the end of my own narrative: *September 13th*.

Dickens had settled into a state of perplexed wonder, and it somewhat perplexed me, as did his gentler, almost fragile, tone of voice. "You see, when I came to revise my *own* story in the proof for the press, the need of a *precise* date was so clear to me, that I inserted in the margin, *September 13th*. The exact same date as mentioned in your account." The wet of his frightened eyes glistened. "How can that be?"

The smell of oils hung unpalatably in the air between us.

"I am profoundly unable to say."

"I mean, could I have heard it from another source? Whom have you told?"

"Not a soul."

"Then have *I* read *your* mind?"

"How is that possible?"

He knew as well as I did that it was not. He prowled some more, picking up my encrusted palette then tossing it down. Lifting my magnifying lens then disregarding it just as sharply.

"I have racked my brains. How I came by it. How it burst the surface. How it flowed from the quill. I remember the delight with which it formed on paper, as it always does. No differently. *No differently*, I say." He peered at me for reassurance, but I could give him none. He saw that and looked away. Moonlight fell on him from the skylight. "It has kept me awake. I sleep like a log. A forest of logs. So what is it? An undesirable bit of beef, a blot of mustard, a crumb of cheese? More of gravy than the grave…?" I recognised the passage he had quoted, but the pun rang a discordant note. More a funeral knell than a chime of Christmas cheer. I knew then that not only did Dickens have no explanation, but this whole affair had shaken him to his core. He was used to being in control at all times, fastidiously so, obsessively so – but this?

He was adamant. "'The Portrait Painter's Story' came from inside my head – I swear it's the truth."

"And mine no less so."

I slid open the top drawer of my plans chest and took out one of the engravings I had made from the drawing in my sketch book. The cross hatching suited the subject of the young woman in repose in the railway compartment. Eliza always urged me not to limit her to a pencil sketch. I peeled back the covering from the print. Dickens let out a cry. The back of his hand attempted to stifle it.

"Dear Christ. It is the same woman I saw in my mind's eye," he said, hushed, as if confiding the most horrible sin. "She was my clay."

"She is not fiction. She was real."

"Real, but not alive."

The writer turned away, shaking his shaggy locks. Looking for escape but finding none, he had no recourse but to turn back to me. "What conjoins us?"

"Madness? I don't wish to contemplate the fact, but I can think of no other."

"There *must* be other! What is the connection between us? We have never met. No two souls could be more different. But there must be a link. There *must* be!" Dickens twisted his head as my wife entered without a knock, asking if we wished for sustenance of any kind. "Tea. Tea is the refresher, the brandisher of swords, the furnace of the spirit. Tea conquers the waves. Tea, my dear, if you please." He was a gunpowder man. Pearl.

"Brandy. Thank you."

When she had gone – "Dead, you say?"

I nodded.

Dickens gave the thinnest of laughs, almost a shudder. "I have always enjoyed the eerie tale. The spectre in the churchyard. The malign influence of the unquiet spirit. The power of the penny dreadful to mesmerise and instruct… I am not enjoying it now." He stared down at his outstretched, trembling hand. "I am as scared as a child. One of the perils of an active imagination." I admired his honesty. We heard the banging of footsteps in the children's bedroom above our heads. We both looked up. "It is past their bed-time."

"I'm sure they have been told so."

"I could go and tell them a story. They tell me I have a knack for such things."

"You'll scare them to death, or have them in tears."

"No. I only reduce adults to tears. When I want to."

The brandy and tea arrived, and Dickens effusively praised my wife in an attempt to make up for his earlier rudeness. A pattern I imagined not to be a rare one. He then pored over the engraving of Caroline Lute as he sipped, and his mood grew more contemplative, if darker, as the moon drifted behind a cloud.

"My concern is this. She visited you to enable you to give her father a likeness of her… but why did she visit *me?* Am I to be tormented like Scrooge until my tormentor gets their way? Am I to be shown some error of my ways? If so, what is it, in the name of God? What can I put right? What is the spectral message I must hear?"

"I do not know." I sighed. "But there are those who converse with the dead. If—"

"I will not go to those people!" Dickens' face contorted in repulsion. "The spirit racket and their ludicrous shenanigans…"

"Where else can you turn?"

"To you," he said, as if visited by a sudden revelation. "You are a seer. Seeing is your profession, after all. You have proven as much, and you will recognise her if we see her again."

"What?"

Revived with the most explosive animation, he shot to his feet and said we must catch a train. Too late now, clearly. He would not travel back to Gad's Hill, but stay at his residence in London overnight. We would meet at noon. No, a quarter past. No – half past one. We could luncheon together, to discuss plans.

"I was intending to have a haircut."

"Then *unintend* it."

He disappeared in a whirl of overcoat, a sense of excitement having replaced his former dread – or what I took to be dread. I hurried to accompany him to the front door but he was already through it. Needles of sleet glinted in the air. The temperature had dropped radically and I heard my teeth chatter.

"Your babes are a-slumber." He noted the silence as he pulled on his gloves, flexing the fingers. "Do you look in and kiss their warm cheeks while they sleep?"

"Always."

Dickens smiled and shook my hand vigorously, holding my eyes as he did so. "Your ghost is mine."

"And yours mine," I said, long before he let go.

* * *

SOME persons, attracted by the lowness of the fare, have an inclination to ride third class, destined to pass the next few hours of their existence tightly compressed between two rough specimens of humanity, but for all his public declamations for social justice, these were not the tickets Dickens acquired. He strode ahead. I had difficulty keeping up. We leapt from platform to locomotive – me breathless, he not – embarking from King's Cross (the old Maiden Lane terminal, as was), steaming up the East Coast route to Retford, via Peterborough. My travelling companion wore an Inverness cape and cheviot trousers, and had hardly compressed his gibus and placed it on the luggage rack before a fellow traveller had identified him, quipping an introductory "God bless us, every one!" before affording himself a self-congratulatory chortle. I had already realised from the many stares we had garnered that Dickens was recognised everywhere – such was the unenviable result of a life lived in the public eye – and for his part, played the role of national figure well, returning a smile and cocked eyebrow in good grace. The man, whose tartan waistcoat was in bitter conflict with its buttons, took this as a signal for conversation, and we were soon regaled with every cherubic charm of his offspring, whose Christmas, it need hardly be added, was made whole and wondrous by the author in whose presence he now found himself. The seat was vacant at Stevenage and Dickens remarked that for all the man's feelings for his own brood, his cufflinks alone would have fed a workhouse boy for a month.

The subject was never far from his thoughts. Children, cruelty, the damage created in our formative years. The roads we are set on. People think of his books as full of mudlarks and pickpockets, snuff-sniffers and chirruping old maids, but the blood that pumped in them at their best was his crusading zeal against inequality; against harm. I think that is why he kept moving. If he stayed still he might see in full the real horror around him.

No sooner had we sat than he had his head down, correcting proofs laid out on his lap. Only as an afterthought did he say he had work to do, and would appreciate quiet in as far as such a thing were possible. I said it was. I looked out of the window as we passed a gang of navvies working on a cutting. One waved his cap, revealing a pink scalp above a brown face. Dickens never looked up.

I took out a pencil and the penny farthing notebook I kept in my inside pocket. A poor likeness, but something of the brooding intensity made it from lead to paper. His was a life of the mind, but he was energised by intellectual curiosity. I had seen how his mental train changed tracks when he saw how to tackle our problem. His security was threatened by things he could not understand, and he meant to put that right. As a painter, on the other hand, I was used to living with abstractions.

Retford is not a busy station. Those who disembark there do so to get somewhere else, not to stop there *per se*. We were therefore the exception. Dickens introduced himself to the station master, one Erasmus Egg, a rotund man with mutton chop whiskers, who straightened his spine as if addressing a commanding officer. His wife, a wren in an eye patch who kept the ticket desk spotless with home comforts, sank to a curtsey. Dickens thanked her but he was not the Prince Consort. She tumbled rather than scurried to the samovar, plying us with digestive biscuits, damson jam, scones, Devon cream, and freshly baked muffins.

"We shall starve," I said.

"He jests. Does he jest?"

"He jests, my dear," said the station master.

Given his surname was Egg I could only pray her Christian name was not Henrietta; the reduction of which to its first syllable would have been a rare affliction. If I were to draw her, I thought at the time, I would have only needed circles.

Dickens wasted no time in saying he was there to investigate details of the disaster that had occurred on 13th September '58. The station master shifted his feet and toyed with a frown.

"For a story?"

"For a story, of sorts," Dickens replied, throwing me a slight sideways glance. "The back issue of *The Times* gives scant account of it."

I noticed the man's wife take out a handkerchief and apply it to her face, scuttling away. Egg apprised us that she had been there, in the thick of it. "Being a former nurse, like. Seeing all sorts, like. Didn't want to, you know, remember, like." The man wiped his palms on the hem of his jacket. I don't know why our faces were anathema, but he chose to look anywhere else. "Eat. Eat! She goes to that much trouble. Too much trouble, I tell her. 'Woman,' I say. 'People need feeding,' she says. Look at me!" He patted his waist. We weren't interested, and neither was he.

"Ahem! Ahem!" He plopped into a chair. A drop of sweat congealed on his upper lip as he told us of the day the goods train hopped the rail. How the passenger train was taking the curve, how the impact took the wheels off the metal. How the carriages tipped and rolled. How the engine itself was a topsy-turvy furnace, coughing coke and fireflies. How the bodies were crushed and scattered. Not bodies. Not all. Not whole.

"We did what we could," he breathed.

"I have no doubt of it," said Dickens, placing a hand on his shoulder.

"I have carried the dead and the dying. I have been at their ear when a priest, by right, should have been."

"That they were not alone in their final moments is a testament to you, not an indictment," said Dickens.

"Excuse me. Did you ever see this woman?" I took the engraved print from the back of my sketch book. He blinked and strangely settled into a mode of resignation, nodding.

"I have seen her since."

"*Since?*"

"So have others. Not clearly. Never clearly. But…" He looked back at the print through sad rather than troubled eyes. "Yes. Her. Often at night. Pale… so very pale. They tease the young apprentices about it. They call her The Lady of the Lines."

An unbecoming part of my anatomy prickled.

Dickens took the picture away, in fear it might upset the poor man further. "How did she die?"

The station master shrugged. "Their faces were covered. Did I tell you? It was all we could do to bring them in from the embankment where they were strewn. We pushed back the furniture. Cleared the floor. They were laid out, in rows," he said, gesturing with a feeble hand to the floorboards we stood on. "Here. In the waiting room."

* * *

THE building having no supply of gas, we were given plentiful candles which we lit and placed upon the table-tops in cups and saucers to light our vigil. I set the filter of the signalling lamp to clear glass – "no danger" – more in vain hope than solid conviction. The night proved foggy and frosty; the windows seemed whitewashed on the outside. Ever restless, Dickens paced past the GNR timetables, back and forth, back and forth. I wondered at times if he sought a misprint or that a wall of type gave him comfort.

"Wainscoting," he said, gazing at the floor then at the ceiling. "Finial… Finial O'Flynn. Phineas Fripp from Frinton-on-Sea. Merchant of alliteration." He walked to the door and back again. "I can't help it. Words buzz around me like flies. I cannot rest till I prise them out of me. Yesterday it was 'irascible'. 'Irascible!'" He adjusted his scarf and his wispy fringe in the mirror. "What a blessing it must be to be simpleminded."

He saw that I was sketching him.

"It pays the bills?"

"I could ask you the same." I smiled.

"Touché," he acknowledged. "Your career, though. I never asked."

No, he hadn't. I told him briefly of my early paintings. Historical. Biblical. That I had learned generally at the knee of my father. That he was an R.A. and expected no less effort than he had applied to his craft. The hours he gave me were hours of failure, by and large. Yet he gave me my trade, whether I wanted it or not.

"Fathers have a lot to answer for." After a few moments he ventured to show another sliver of curiosity. "Your charming wife."

"Eliza."

"And tumbling, tow-headed children. How many?"

"Just the two."

"Tsk! You've barely started. Fill the house with them."

"Our house is full already. With noise, anyway."

"The best noise in the world."

He displayed no obvious sadness on the surface, but I knew, as everyone did from the newspapers, that he was separated from his wife, and though he had custody of his children, under the guardianship of Georgina, their aunt, his eldest had chosen to live with his mother.

"I too have a son named Charlie," I said.

Dickens looked at me with a deeper gratitude than the statement warranted.

"She had become mad, you see. I had no choice. Five hundred pounds a year is no pittance. Did she want my blood? In exchange for what? Her child-bearing years? Was my cheque book not enough?" I thought very probably not. His expression became clouded, perhaps with guilt, perhaps with self-pity. Why he sought to justify himself to me I had no idea. "Her presence had become a distraction. From the work. You see?" I could not say that I did. What work was more important than being a father and husband? But perhaps I thought that because I was incapable of being a Great Man. If so, I was happy with that.

Dickens took out a Dutch pipe and filled it with dark leaf Syrian latakia.

"Thomas…"

"My wife calls me Frank."

"Then Frank it is," he said, striking a match and soon as swathed in smoke as any locomotive. And what followed, to my astonishment, was the approximation of an apology. "You wrote under your own name from your own address. There was no doubt in you being a responsible gentleman; it became my duty to read your communication attentively and without delay. I regret any injustice my suspicious mind and manner may have conveyed."

"We are who we are."

"Indeed." He scanned the room, its mahogany lightened by flower vases only adding to the impression of a funeral parlour. The grand clock ticked its wagging finger. "As a child my nanny scared me with bugaboo tales. Savages. Torture. Pirates…"

"Like the station master's wife?"

Recalling the eye patch Dickens laughed, expelling a grey, bulbous cloud. "I imbibed *The Terrific Register*, with its catalogue of cannibalism, death, murder, and above all—"

"Ghosts."

"It led, unforgivably – or forgivably – to a hankering for, and interest in, all things supernatural."

"Yet you ridicule the séance room."

He drummed the table top with his knuckles. "Two knocks for yes. Three knocks for no. Five knocks for how's your father. Bark if you recognise Uncle Tom. Where was Moses when the lights went out? Ringing a bell or blowing a horn? Do the clowns not ask for it?"

"The grief-stricken are not clowns."

His pipe stem stabbed at the air between us. "And there you have my repugnance in a nutshell." He leaned back in the upholstered creak of the chair, an ethereal swirl of tobacco rising, enveloping, as he sucked. "But for the strong restraining power of common sense, I might have fallen into a belief in such follies. As it was, the fanciful side of my nature stopped short at such superstitions as luck and fortuitous dreams, and marvels such as coincidence and earthbound spirits." The irony escaped neither of us. "No man was ever readier to apply sharp tests to a story of a ghost or haunted house, even as I demanded absolute credence when I told them."

"A contradiction?"

"Not at all. An author is not bound by legal contract to believe what he writes. We would all be the poorer if he were. Therein lies the task, as I see it. To make the

downright impossible feel, if for but a minute, for a page –
for a *book* – more real than the world at the reader's elbow."

"So you hold no fear of ghosts?"

"I hold no *fear*—" The great lion, chin on chest, listened
to the brittle hush of the stove and considered his response
carefully: "Let us say… I prefer my lost souls shackled to
the printed page."

"Tonight I don't think we have a choice."

An hour later it was me doing the pacing. I said
something about feeling uncomfortable walking over the
spot where those who had been killed had been lain out.
Without looking up, Dickens said we tread on memories
every day. I said, nevertheless, it felt like sacrilege. He
asked would it be less so, had we not been told? He recalled
he had walked many a church aisle and seldom thought of
those buried beneath – though on occasion, as a child, had
taken charcoal rubbings of their names and dates. His first
gateways to other lives. Lives imagined. "Their secrets
and injustices, their hopes and prayers. A mother and son.
A man and wife. I'd pick up my copy book and put flesh
on the bones."

I stared at the mopped and bleached floorboards.
I felt my skin was bleached too. I scratched my cheek,
continuing my perambulations.

The clock struck twelve.

I spotted a pack of cards, either provided for the
entertainment of journeyers whiling their time at this
inauspicious interchange, or else left behind by one of the
aforementioned themselves.

I sat, shuffled, and dealt for a game of Beat the Knave
Out o' Doors, the only card game that Pip knew how to
play in *Great Expectations*, Dickens' big success of the
summer just past. Eliza had consumed it voraciously. I
enjoyed more seeing the delight in her face as she turned
each page.

"We crave them," he mused. "They appear. Why do
they appear? Is it their longing, or ours?

"The public itch to be spooked, and you oblige them. Does that make you better than a medium? You take money for your ghosts too."

"I never espouse that they are real."

"And now?"

"Now is the perfect end to a chapter," he said.

"If only. But here we sit. The chapter is not over. Nor the tale."

I shuffled the cards again and dealt a second time.

The windows grew more densely opaque. As natural darkness, at close of day, bathes the earth in an ever deeper black, so, in a peculiar and unsettling manner, an ever thickening *whiteness* seemed to surround us that night.

Strip Jack Naked is not a game of tremendous skill. Even so, Dickens' mind was not on it. Distracted, and now bored, he scraped at the embers in his pipe with a sterling silver cleaner, but they would not relight. The shoulders sagged, weighty with yesteryear. The pipe hung from the hand, which hung from his knee.

"I once attended a séance in Berkeley Square. The lamp was turned low and I heard a female voice. I recognised my sweet, dead sister – Fanny. Dear Fan…" An unmistakable scar of memory flickered across the writer's features, tempered by a feather-touch of joy. "It was even a song she sang. The dark was never so filled with prettiness, nor my eyes so gushing in thanks. Then a sergeant's hand shot out and grabbed the wrist of a whippersnapper cursing to the four winds. The gas came up on the most dissolute exposure. A boy in silk, his wig half off. A rapping machine attached to the underside of the table. Cheesecloth hidden in orifices it does not care to specify." He placed the Dutch pipe next to the signalling lantern and picked strands of leaf from his fingers. "I was enraged. I so *wanted* it, you see. And there they have you. The hook of the *want*. Not even the strongest pike can escape it."

"But is there more than this?" By which I meant the material world around us. "Surely a perfectly legitimate question?"

"Not if answered by tricksters and criminals."

"One of my greatest joys is painting the impression of light. Sometimes I think to myself, we are the paint, but we are not the light. We are simply the rendering."

Dickens said nothing. At least he did not grunt, though I am not saying he wasn't tempted. I took the print from the back of my sketch book, and placed it on the table between us.

"She needed your artist's eye. Our unwanted muse. If anyone can answer our questions, it is she."

"Will it bring her?"

"I have no idea," he said.

"Shall we join hands?"

"I think not."

Mine were in prayer and I blew into them. They had become icy, wrapped up though we were. I had trod on the Cairngorms in the thick of winter and the weather had been more temperate. I dug in my pocket and took out a hip flask. The malt would warm us at least. Dickens partook of it eagerly. It robbed him of breath. He said, not inaccurately, it had "more of the thistle than the heather."

A minute later his thoughts turned back to matters ghostly.

"Once a spiritualist said my creative talent was akin to psychic ability, if I but knew it." He laughed, loudly and scornfully. "They'd love to get me in their tribe!"

"Perhaps that is not as ludicrous as it sounds." I upended the hip flask and took a second mouthful, which burned my gums but sharpened my brain. "You said yourself how the image of her burst the surface unbidden. How it flowed onto the page with you as its… well, yes – *medium*. What if you were to put yourself into the same enraptured, *entranced* state you experience when writing?"

"Will it help us see her?"

"It helped you see her before."

He could not deny that was a fact. He reached out to me – I thought, ridiculously, for my hand, but in fact it was for the hip flask. Pattison's Morning Dew did its job. The Scotch hit the back of his throat.

"*Talitha cumi*," he whispered. "Quickly—" Though why *quickly* I do not know; the dead, in as far as I know, do not keep a strict timetable of appearances.

He bade me fetch the blackboard hung near the door to the platform, used by the station master to habitually scrawl messages such as the one it still displayed: YORK TRAIN DELAYED: COW ON TRACKS. At his instruction, I laid it across his lap like a breakfast tray, resting it on the arms of the chair. I understood then what he was doing; we had to recreate the circumstances of his daily occupation. It was a substitute for his writing desk.

He opened his carpet bag and extracted a travelling ink set, which included a Bohemian threaded glass ink well in a leather case with rounded edges, and a three-section mother of pearl dipping pen with four nibs. These he assembled and arranged with the precision of a surgeon, though he said it was sorely inadequate to reproduce his writing habits with precise exactitude; his usual paper was not to hand, nor his goose quill, nor the surrounding beds and sofas – which had to be all placed in every detail according to the author's meticulous eye. The sturdy iron stove was poor imitation of his home fire back in Kent, but still – as he rolled back his shirt cuffs and unscrewed a bottle of Blackwood & Co. writing fluid – it would have to do.

For some reason I was minded to turn the filter in the signalling lantern to red; something to do with mediums operating all the better in dim light. I had done it before I questioned it, and by the time I had, my companion's nib was hovering over the blank sheet I'd torn from my sketch pad and placed on what amounted to his makeshift drawing board, next to the print of the young woman from the railway carriage.

"Caroline… sweet child," said he, scribbling down her name then shutting his eyes. "Caroline *Lute*. The most plaintive of instruments. Such beauty. Such sorrow. May we hear your music this night, Miss Lute?"

I said nothing as he took several very deep breaths, holding them on the intake.

The pen did not lift from the paper, but remained held there, making only the most miniscule movements – a tiny scratch here, a twitch there, the angle of its mast adjusting – as if waiting to be compelled to do so.

"You are a mystery. And every writer has to know the answer to the mystery before he begins." Dickens took two more breaths, deeper than the first. The red light shone like blood on one side of his face. His eyebrows arched. His thinking almost visible… "What were you doing on the train, my dear? Why were you alone? A young lady travelling with no husband, no chaperone? Where were you going – and why? That is your story. What were you fleeing from… or to?" He tilted his head, waiting for the reply to come on the metaphorical or actual ether. As perhaps he did when composing his characters. "Had you loved? Or been loved?"

Answer came there none.

I could not see how there could, but in another way I prayed that we would get… something. That tiny movement of her head as she left the train came back to me.

We shall meet again.

I thought then: *How? How can we? How are such things possible?*

I was terrified I would soon find out.

Meanwhile Dickens listened to the silence. I saw no fragment of impatience in his face. He had sunk into another realm; I think even become another Dickens. The bodily one had left him. The pen-smith was all, now.

"Why would a woman travel alone?" His frown disappeared. "Ah, but you were not alone. There was another with you." A smile slowly came to his lips. "That's it. I see it now. My friend told me how you kept your fur on your lap. How you were covered in layers. Was it to prevent a lump being noticed? The life you carried inside? Ah, yes! *Yes!* He said you wore no wedding ring. Of course! You are on your way to tell the baby's father. He doesn't know yet, does he, on that September 13th? The man who might embrace you and marry you or refuse to even see you? *No!* A man who has a wife and children already. Is that it? A man of whom your father would never approve. A man about whom you can never tell him. And so you sit on the train, facing a future that terrifies you – that you hardly know how to face. The loss of your family, the loss of your reputation, the shame, the rejection, and then—*THEN*—"

Dickens turned to stone, his limbs stiffening.

I took away the board and placed it on the floor, half on top of his bag.

His hand did not falter. It held the pen in mid-air.

"Go on. Go on."

I watched as a ghastly pallor drained his features. His breath quickened with alarm and he convulsed, no less than if he were being stabbed by unseen spears.

He suddenly stood up, poker-straight, eyes remaining shut – but now as if he was willing them to fight against their natural instinct to spring open.

"Did you not hear it? The piercing shriek of the wheels torn from the rail! The awful silence before the endless thrashing of mangled metal! Then, dear Lord above, the sickening hissing of the slaughtered engine, the roar reduced not even to a purr… and *now,* like the most base insult to humanity, rising, there come the cries – not *screams,* but more pitiable *by far* than that – the *moans,* the powerless wails of unimaginable pain. Guttural calls in the dark of night to their invisible Maker. Isolated voices as stars in the heavens… each one pleading from throats clogged with blood for help as shallow life ebbs away – Do you hear them? *Do you hear them now?*" Dickens dropped the pen and reached out with both hands to find my lapels. "Tell me you do! *In the name of God, tell me you do!*"

"I hear nothing. There is nothing!"

Terrified by the look on his face, I shook him hard, but he would not wake, which terrified me all the more.

He rocked, as I have only seen Quakers do when the spirit moves them.

Still with his eyes closed, he said: "I see her!"

Only then did he open them.

"I see her!" he said again, unblinking – his gaze fixed at something over my left shoulder.

I turned, bending to lift the signal man's lamp from the table as I did so, though what I saw did not require the light to fall upon it. In fact, no light did. It was content in its own shadowy reality, untouched, and could not be touched any more than the figure in a Daguerrotype could be – even by light. The most fundamental component of the physical, and so beloved of my art school tutors – *light and shade.*

Framed by the glazed double-doors behind her, with the roiling mist beyond, she stood, looking exactly as she had done when I first saw her in the railway compartment. The same furs, dress, ankle-length coat. The button-up shoes buffed to a shine. The hat with a veil – which, as she had before, she lifted away from her pale countenance with coy but exquisite reluctance. This time, however, I read in her troubled, downcast eyes the narrative that Dickens had intuited. She smiled only, I felt, to remind me of her unearthly promise.

We shall meet again.

It had been amusing, odd, strange – but now was fulfilled. I felt a blockage in my throat.

She looked down at the rabbit-skin muff she held against her stomach. I saw now that it was not a muff at all but rather a swaddling blanket, and that nestling within it slept a newborn babe.

A sharp bang made me turn away. The Dutch pipe had rolled off the table and lay on the floor. The tiny embers it spilled glowed brightly then faded almost at once. I looked up into Dickens' face and beheld a man in the grip of shock.

I looked back at the phantom.

The woman said with unparalleled sorrow: "Could you not touch me, Papa?"

Now it was the sound of a sob that made me turn. I could not believe that it had come from Dickens, but it had. I do not think his critics often thought him either mute or powerless but those two qualities overwhelmed him then. For the first time I saw in him the boy in the boot blacking factory. Hopeless, frightened, small.

Withered, he walked – no, staggered – past me, like a man in a dream.

The young woman's smile did not waver as he neared her. She merely looked down gently as Dickens placed his hand on the baby's head, the great meat of life on a perfect, pink skull that had seen none of it. He leaned over and kissed the child's forehead.

Behind me the door to the platform sprang open as some devilish behemoth howled and my blood turned to ice. Smoke or steam or mist rolled in as a locomotive clattered through the station at high speed without stopping, its horn blaring. The sudden displacement of air must have nudged the door off its latch. The draught caught the angled board upon which Dickens had been writing, and his ink well slid off it onto the floorboards, making a puddle which resembled a splash of blood.

I quickly looked back.

Dickens had turned towards the sound, sallow eyed, and towards me. The cold air from the door raked through his stray locks.

The figures of the young woman and the child were both gone. So too, in the next instant, was the rattling of the milk train, leaving us nothing but its whirling, slicing echo, and thereafter only a welcome but all-consuming quietude.

* * *

THE large clock mounted on the wall showed half past five. My pocket watch was slow, or it was fast. Not that it mattered. I turned the signalling lamp to 'clear' and turned up the wick. The stain on the floor looked a lot less like blood when it was seen to be blue. I picked up the mother of pearl pen, dismantled it and packed it away in the travelling case.

Dickens sat with his elbows on his knees, a lifeless effigy awaiting Guy Fawkes Night, shoulders hunched, head slumped, uncharacteristically void of conversation, or even action. Little as I knew him, he worried me in such a state. With few weapons in my arsenal, I offered the hip flask again.

He waved it away with a flicker of disdain.

"The travel clock shows half past nine," I said, holding said object, for the sake of something to say. "The time of the crash was half past nine. Maria Lute told me. I didn't put in it my account. You said it kept good time."

Dickens did not answer. Nor did he look at me.

"You do not beckon love," he said, apropos of nothing. "Love beckons you. It seizes your heart, or grows there. There can be no will to resist it. It is a truth that can only be denied, and to deny it is a betrayal of our nature." He now seemed to want to shrink away from me. "Ellen was an actress. Is no longer. We had to be discreet, you see. Of necessity. I was a married man. I had a reputation. Children. Many who would by hurt by the knowledge of such a person… such a thing. It could not be seen, but it had to continue. We could not resist the pull of it."

"Sir—"

I did not want to hear what was clearly agonizing to get out, but his eyes narrowed and his firmness told me he wanted his say.

"It died, you see. Our child. On that summer's eve. Two days it lived and breathed. I tell you, more did it suffer in those forty-eight hours on earth than in my forty-nine years. And when it lay in its cot, cold and still… I could not touch it." Now – *now* he looked at me. "Not a living soul could know such a thing. None but a dead one." His voice quivered. His lip twisted. "That is why those charlatans who pretend they can…"

I could say nothing.

"Perhaps we should have gone to one," he continued. "Ellen wanted to. I said no. 'Death is death, the child is gone. It is not to be endured. *Life* is to be endured.' She said: 'You pretend he was nothing, but he was our son.'" Here he broke, and his body shook with the pain he had held inside for so long. "Why could I not touch him? *Why could I not?* And why do we need the dead to instruct us?"

I did not know.

I did not know the answer to any of it. Just as I could not know the extent of his shame or his guilt. All I did know, now, was that the ghost had visited Dickens, as it had visited me, for a reason. And though I saw tears rolling down his cheeks and falling onto those floorboards where the dead had been given their last resting place, I somehow knew a weight had been lifted. A great weight, lifted by something as unsubstantial as a feather, a quill, as air, as a memory, as a prayer.

* * *

THE mist lifted and the day arrived like scenery sailed in from the wings. Dickens was revived in spirit, or seemed to be. We had not slept, but soon after dawn had taken ourselves for breakfast at the Swan Hotel. It was no time to regale Dickens with my misgivings about provincial fare and, in fairness, the cooking did not poison us. He indulged in more boiled eggs than seemed wise for the human constitution and I hoped he had taken into account the probable effects of a long journey on his digestive tract. For one in a sedentary profession, he devoured food in a way that made me wonder why he didn't have a belly the size of Mr Pickwick, but I think his energy burned it away with the ferocity of a forest fire.

We reached the station to find Mr and Mrs Egg in their allotted roles. Too many *eggs* for one morning, I thought to myself. The samovar bubbled. We partook of more tea. There was always space for more tea; we were Englishmen, after all. The station master asked if anything had happened during the night. "Anything – *ghostly*, like." Before I could answer, Dickens, lifting his carpet bag, said that there had not.

"Well. Oh, well. We shall keep you posted if we see the lassie again."

"Do. If you address your envelope to *Dickens, London* it usually gets to me. Thank you for the candles. And thank you for the tea. Both were efficacious."

The two of us made our way to the platform to await the train from York to London. I couldn't help considering what the events that had occurred might mean to my companion in the future. "A woman on a train, travelling alone to tell the father of her child that she is expecting. That's a story for you."

"No, that's *her* story," Dickens said, tugging on his gloves. "It is enough that we know it. Perhaps, with God's blessing, that will be her release." He craned forward, staring towards the end of the track, the better to spot our train approaching. Perhaps he was eager to rejoin the metropolitan throng. I could not read his thoughts. Such territory belonged to mystics and clairvoyants. Though it was a territory we had ventured into ourselves, if only for a passing overnight visit. I should not wish to live there.

"The public do not need to know the mistakes and wounds of fallible men," he said without meeting my eyes. "Enough for them to enjoy from me a tall tale or two."

I understood he wanted me to keep his secret. Of the mistress. Of their love. Of the child they had lost. And I would. Until now, when all those who might have been hurt by it are gone, and can be hurt no more.

Before long we were joined by others, the platform filling with a steady stream of passengers, all with their little voyages to make, be it the trudge to factory or office, a visit to an ailing relative or needy child. All had their stories. All stood preoccupied with them, oblivious to the invisible world around them, a world beyond the foibles and unfairnesses of Man, where spirits remind us of our flaws or ask our help even as they plague and terrify us. Perhaps we deserve no less. I was made no happier by having those thoughts in my mind, and envied those who didn't. I want to paint every glorious, ignorant one of them.

Once we had found our compartment, Dickens immersed himself in his papers, dragging the page proofs onto his knees once more, head down, blind to my presence as I knew he would be.

At one point, though, he looked up, after a few moments of thought, and said: "The ghost has done her duty."

"She has."

"I think she is at peace now."

"I think so too," I said.

I was tempted to draw him, and if I had, I think I would have drawn a different Dickens on my return journey than I had on the way up. I chose not to, and instead closed my eyes and let sleep's balm engulf me. It was sorely needed and my lids were heavy. But with slumber came a picture in my mind's eye. That of Dickens, kneeling to place flowers on a tiny, unmarked grave. It brought to mind an inscription on a headstone I had once seen when flitting through a churchyard as a boy: THOSE WHO HAVE BEEN LOVED, THEY SHALL NOT DIE.

Those who have been loved, they shall not die.

I opened my eyes, looked at Dickens and smiled.

"Go back to sleep," he said. "I'm working."

❖

Incredibly, "The Waiting Room" was inspired by a true ghost story involving Charles Dickens. His tale "A Portrait Painter's Story" first appeared in a journal he edited, All the Year Round, in September 1861. Immediately after publication, Thomas Frank Heaphy, an artist, wrote to the author claiming that the protagonist, who encountered a ghostly woman on a train had been, in fact, himself. Furthermore, he could prove it, because he had sent an exact account of his preternatural experience to a rival magazine.

Dickens was shocked by the bizarre coincidence. He called the episode "so very original, so very extraordinary, so very far beyond the version I have published that all stories turn pale before it." In the absence of any rational explanation, the two men eventually reached an agreement; Heaphy's MS appeared in the October issue of Dickens' All the Year Round. It was later reprinted, alongside the correspondence between painter and author, as "A Wonderful Ghost Story Being Mr H's Own Narrative" (price one shilling).

Four years later, in 1865, Dickens was involved in the Staplehurst train crash, during which several carriages plummeted into the Beult River. Many say it was the inspiration for his story "The Signal Man" – one of the most revered ghost stories in the English language. Five years after it, Dickens himself was dead, and his son said in his eulogy that his father had never fully recovered from the trauma of the accident. So perhaps the cries he heard in the waiting room at Retford Junction were not an echo of the past – but of the future? An ill portent of Tragedy Yet To Come?

One thing is true. That the events surrounding 'A Portrait Painter's Story' did nothing to diminish Victorian England's most celebrated wordsmith's interest in the supernatural. A year later, The Ghost Club was founded in London, and Dickens became one of its most pre-eminent and active members.

SV

Christmas Eve, 2020

Charles, Greene & Parkinson

Foxhill Dr., Northolt

This one-of-a-kind SHUG MONKEY is the ideal first pet for your little monkey. Available now from:

CHALLENGER'S
West Wratting

The Confirmed Bachelors

1

IT should be stated at the outset, for those who expect a certain kind of thing from a certain kind of tale, that, when investigating Arilda House in his capacity as a member of the Society for Psychical Research, Flaxton found no evidence, let alone proof, of a haunting. Not that he especially *sought* a preternatural explanation, nor did he – God forbid – leap to grasp any tenuous thread that might be clung to in that regard. Such lack of discipline would entirely go against the grain of his essentially sceptical nature. However, it must be said, and he almost *did* say, the place certainly looked the part, with two sharply-angled rooves and a trio of chimney stacks nestled in a small copse of trees surrounded by a patchwork quilt of fields, the nearest sizeable place of habitation being Oldbury-on-Severn, which had emerged around a tidal inlet called 'The Pill', the muddy waters of which marked, and still mark,

59

the centre of the village. Flaxton had absorbed from the five or six pages of correspondence, and was grateful to have done, a little of the building's history. Notably, it had been used as a sanitarium for British officers during the war years until the Armistice in November 1918, subsequent to which it returned to its role as a comfortable private home, and he could see immediately, upon arrival, how children, or a child, at least, would take great joy in sliding down the wonderful banisters. No doubt installed at great expense by Brinsley Boxall, founder of the London and Hibernian Bank, who had built it in 1889 as a summer residence.

The tumulus upon which the adjacent church sat, something of a local landmark offering fine views of the estuary, was of inexact but almost certainly pre-Christian origin. Roman coins had been found in the graveyard, a mere stone's throw from the former rectory's windswept garden, half of which was canopied by a modern conservatory. It did not require great imagination to picture therein convalescing servicemen stretched out on loungers, exchanging Woodbines. 'Arilda' – the name of house and church alike – came from that of a local saint from Saxon times, the little known of her having been recorded by the historian Leland: "Saynt Arild Vergin, martyred at Kineton ny Thornberye by one Muncius a tiraunt, who cut off hir heade becawse she would not consent to lye with him." The unfortunate martyr had later been buried in the crypt of Gloucester Cathedral, the only other church dedicated to her being Oldbury-on-the-Hill, only about fifteen miles away. Having imparted this information, which he called his 'homework', to the lady of the house, Flaxton found his conversation ran onto embarrassingly stony ground. Talking to the fairer sex being something at which he could not even pretend to be particularly accomplished.

He took out his pocket watch, not for the first time, and politely refused a chair in favour of pacing to the front door and back, yet again. To Flaxton tardiness bordered on selfish lack of consideration. He knew he should be tolerant, and relaxed – there is nothing one can do, after all, about the flaws of another human being – but he couldn't help it. He found it unbearable.

Until, that is, they heard a car's approach; the same taxi that had brought Flaxton an hour and a half earlier. Pomeroy swept in wearing a camel jacket with velvet collar and bleached quarry trousers, the familiar ever-rumpled fawn raincoat open and flowing. He sported a boater, which he quickly deposited on a nearby hook, and full brogue brown and white spectator shoes. Flaxton thought he looked as if he was on his way to the Henley Regatta. It made him feel self-consciously dull in his pinstripe.

"Flaxton."

"Pomeroy."

"Old bean."

A handshake was superfluous to requirements. The taxi driver huffed and puffed as he brought in various boxes, suitcases, tripods, and camera equipment, some of which Flaxton recognized, some of which he did not. Pomeroy apologized for his delay, saying there had been an uncoupling at Temple Meads.

"Flaxton."
"Pomeroy."

"I took an earlier train, to be on the safe side," said Flaxton.

"Of course you did."

The woman of the house extended a hand which the newcomer took even more limply than it was offered.

"Mr Pomeroy. Hello. I recognize you from the *Daily Mail*."

"That is no great recommendation, I fear."

"Thousands would agree," said Flaxton, matching his colleague's smile, if thinly.

The famed 'Ghost Seeker' had been all too visible in the popular press recently with photographs taken at his Laboratory for Psychic Education in Wembley whilst testing the extrasensory powers of a young German medium. Pomeroy had been quoted in the *Mail* as saying that during these experiments he had been witness to extraordinary feats – the moving of objects under séance conditions; material manifestations caught on film; messages from the beyond that had been subsequently authenticated. Flaxton himself was not sure that the information could not have been obtained by a jungle telegraph of informers, but Pomeroy insisted that any communication was via the ether itself, "by some method we have yet to understand". He'd told Flaxton "he was an extraordinary boy" and on that he staked his reputation. As what, Flaxton was by no means sure. As a scientist, he supposed.

"Professor Flaxton is just as well-regarded in his own field. A respected academic, as I'm sure he has told you."

"I'm afraid he has rather hidden his own light under a bushel."

"Then I shall lift that bushel off, forthwith." Pomeroy's lips covered crooked teeth but he smiled without effort.

Flaxton's cheeks reddened. He cursed that it had been drilled into him never to crow about one's accomplishments. In the middle-class Colchester of his parents, to show off was the most grievous sin imaginable. But in the present circumstances he had no reason to be coy. After all, his scholarly achievements were considerable. He had been lauded by his peers, and published extensively, yet to the public mind it was Pomeroy's name that was synonymous with the scientific study of the psychical – not his. Granted, Pomeroy had dedicated his life to it, as he was fond of saying, and in so doing attracted publicity, or courted it, thought Flaxton from his ivory tower. But, whilst dismissing any desire for wide recognition by the hoi polloi as crass, if not downright vulgar, he could not deny the merest sliver of envy.

Introductions were in order. Firstly to Mrs Dulcie Willett, then her daughter, Lizzy-May. The freckled twelve-year-old curtsied somewhat over-dramatically in her pinafore dress and blouse with a lace trim at the collar, her hair cut short into a bubbly halo of curls.

"Delightful."

"Don't be deceived." An older, ample woman worked at the range. "She's a terror, that one."

The child laughed, skipped over and pulled undone the bow of the cook's apron.

"Mrs Ready has her work cut out with us," said her mother, betraying a Yorkshire accent in the way she pronounced *us*. "But she's a godsend, and bakes like an angel. Scones are in the oven. The Professor's tea cup is empty. Are you ready for a fresh brew?"

"I would rather see the offending room first, if we may? Flaxton, if you'd be so kind."

"Certainly, old chap."

"Jolly-ho."

The two men gathered what luggage they could carry in both arms and made their way up the staircase which creaked admirably with every footfall. Lizzy-May carried Flaxton's own overnight bag and her mother brought up the rear.

"The master bedroom is on the right."

Lizzy-May tugged the Professor's hand as soon as he reached the landing. "Come and see *my* room!" He could hardy refuse, could he?

The child's enclave was sizeable, more sizeable than the one he'd occupied in Colchester. Affecting approval of the nursery wallpaper and a silver-maned rocking horse which he nudged into motion, Flaxton looked over the net curtain into an overgrown patch of lawn and shrubbery, where he saw a wheelbarrow lying on its side next to a broken flowerpot. He could not help noticing the picture book on the bedside table near his left hand. Its green cover showed an illustration of flying imps with butterfly wings cavorting in a tangle of thorns and petals.

"A fairy book," he laughed. "Do you have fairies at the bottom of your garden?"

"Fairies and ghosts?" The girl threw herself onto her bed. "That would be silly!"

Flaxton placed the book down and saw a framed photograph beside it of a man in an army uniform. An officer, possibly a major.

"This is Fluffy Tonks." Lizzy-May held out a moth-eaten teddy bear. "Mother says I'm too old for him. Am I?"

"I don't think anybody's too old for Fluffy Tonks."

By the time Flaxton had entered the bedroom in question – the *offending* bedroom – Pomeroy had brought up the remaining boxes and was already setting up his artefacts. Of the two tripods, one was for the Adams and Co. Reflex Camera that used infra-red film (a necessity for night photography), the other for the Kodak Brownie Model F using conventional film, which Pomeroy screwed into place in its landscape iteration. A thermograph designed to be triggered by changes in temperature or movement waited to be primed. Furthermore a brass-cased desktop barometer with silvered dial (marked 'stormy' to 'variable', with various calibrations around its circumference) sat on the sideboard, courtesy of a fold-out easel stand. Flaxton also recognised – and described to Mrs Willett – the Robinson anemometer, consisting as it did of four hemispherical cups on horizontal arms mounted on a vertical shaft. The air flowing past the cups turned the shaft at a rate proportional to the air's speed. Therefore, any invisible influence would be detected as a rotational force.

Mrs Willett nodded, giving the pretence of interest, but Flaxton was unconvinced.

As Lizzy-May yanked her arm on some pretext or other – *demanding child* – Flaxton caught sight of a framed picture beside the four-poster, similar to the one he'd seen in the other bedroom. A man and wife on their wedding day. Same man. Same uniform. Lest the woman notice him spotting it, he looked away, feigning a survey of the room in general, focusing his interest, though he had none, on an embroidery sampler with a quote ascribed to the poet Swinburne:

> *Above the sea and sea-washed town we dwelt,*
> *We twain together, two brief summers, free*

He coughed into his hand.

Mrs Willett stood with her arms crossed, her daughter resting her head against her mother's elbow.

"Old chap."

"Old boy."

Pomeroy always brought a sketch book and pencils, and their immediate task was to draw a layout plan of the room with exact measurements made with a metallic tape measure from his ghost hunter's tool kit. Flaxton concentrated on holding the end of the tape as Pomeroy called out the feet and inches, which Flaxton punctiliously noted. Punctiliousness being his forte.

"Original beams?"

"Original woodworm," answered Mrs Willett. Flaxton observed she wore short sleeves and her pale unblemished skin looked frozen. He was relieved when she took a cardigan from a drawer and put it on.

Presently Pomeroy circled the room, rapping the whitewashed walls with his knuckles, the alteration in sound telling him the plaster was blown in places. His eyes telling him it was cracked in others.

"Natural movement over the years," said Mrs Willett. "Not *un*natural, let us assume."

Pomeroy rose to the tips of his toes, then bent his knees, testing the spring in the floor, which was considerable, even given the age of the property, so that was noted too. He then arranged his rolls of adhesive tape which would be used to seal the room once the duo were ensconced. To keep out draughts, and to make any human interference evident if the seals were broken. Yes, Pomeroy was a believer – but he also believed in fakery. And it had to be ruled out. That was one thing upon which he and Flaxton agreed.

Mrs Willett plucked a stray feather from the throw and leaned over to puff the pillows, but generally, throughout the two men's preparations, kept a distance from the bed as if in the presence of a securely chained but potentially violent beast. The reason for such behaviour had been fully described in her letter to the SPR; her experience of being wakened, and then *kept* awake, over weeks, and now months, by the 'bucking bed' as she termed it – *levitation* being the term the scientists would use, though the image of a horse trying to throw its rider remained a powerful one, and in dead of night, no doubt a terrifying one.

Flaxton examined the carvings on the bedposts, knowing his colleague would very likely photograph them in close-up detail later. The heraldic shields reminded him of brass rubbings he had made as a lad. Wyverns, talbots, arrow-heads and fleurs-de-lis. Reminiscent of cub scout badges and whatnot, he thought.

"16th century. Fit for a king."

"But the house is not 16th century," opined his colleague.

"The man from the Parochial Church Council said as much." Mrs Willett's letter had explained the family had benefitted from the decision by the executive bodies of the Church of England to sell properties that were expensive to maintain and a drain on funds. "The bed must have come from elsewhere. Somebody took a liking to it. One of the old vicars, presumably. I never did. All that dark wood absorbing the light, making the room gloomy…"

"Oak," said Flaxton.

"Any rate, it was too big to get down the stairs without taking it apart. I wouldn't have minded that. Might've made good firewood. The man joked it came with the property, like the rodents."

"Scratch, scratch." Lizzy-May flexed her fingers and wrinkled her nose.

"Yes. Which reminds me. Mind the traps," warned her mother.

"I don't mind them," said Lizzy-May.

"Brave girl," said Flaxton.

"Mice don't hurt you."

Flaxton got the distinct impression she might have meant other things did.

Pomeroy tested the mattress.

"Comfortable?"

"When I used to sleep in it. Before things started."

"It always strikes me how people were much shorter in those days."

"Didn't they used to dress up to go to bed, also?"

"Probably."

"Teeth a-chatter," said Flaxton. "A devil to find a way to keep yourself warm. I mean, er…" He didn't know what he did mean, in truth, or why the back of his neck had become hot. It was a dashed nuisance.

"How many people have died in beds?" Pomeroy folded back the top blanket at one corner. "Yet so few are haunted. The linen's clean. You keep an immaculate home."

"As I say, Mrs Ready is a godsend."

"Ah! Whilst I think of it, would you do the honours?" Pomeroy dashed over to his Brownie. He had already taken the roll of film out of the foil packet and loaded it onto the spool. It was just a case of winding it on. He positioned Mrs Willett behind the camera, facing the bed. "Turn the knob clockwise until you see the next number in the window. Then click the little silver lever down. Just here, look."

Pomeroy leapt into bed, fully clothed, dragging the top blanket over his midriff. "Come along, Flaxton, shake a leg, old man!"

"All right! Gracious me. What a nag you are." Flaxton climbed in beside him, the two of them sitting up in their finery. Pinstripe suit. Camel jacket. Waistcoats with a strain on the buttons. Stiff collars. Staring at the camera lens.

"Say cheese."

"Certainly not," said Flaxton. "Stuff and nonsense."

Mrs Willett clicked the shutter.

"Move it on and take another. I feel 'me laddo' was rather too animated."

"Oh, very nice."

"Well you don't want to come out a blur."

"Perhaps I do."

The woman gazed down into the viewfinder. "You know, in the 19th century, before they used 'Say cheese', photographers used to ask their clients to say 'Plum and pickle'."

"You learn something new every day," mumbled Flaxton.

"Plum and pickle!" cried Pomeroy, holding the grin, and after the click was heard, "Bravo! One more for luck if you please, my dear. Thank you."

Click!

"Do you like my ribbons? Do you like green or do you like red?" Lizzy-May held up coloured strands of cloth either side of her head above her ears. Flaxton had not even seen her raiding her mother's sewing box.

"The gentlemen are not here to talk about your ribbons, Lizzy-May."

"Oh, I rather think we are, aren't we, Flaxton?"

"Oh, indeed, Pomeroy. I say red."

"I say red too."

Seemingly pleased with that decision, the little girl skipped out of the room and they heard her footsteps in button boots pattering down the staircase. Mrs Willett flickered a smile of apology. Flaxton's told her it was not needed.

"Right then. Let the dog see the rabbit." Pomeroy got out of his side of the bed, tweaked his trousers above the knee, and bent over, gripping the frame. Flaxton took his instruction as implicit and did the same on his side. "One, two, three." They attempted to lift it, and failed.

Flaxton stood up, straightening his back with a groan. "Shaking this blighter would take four men at least."

"Or one ghost," said Mrs Willett – without the slightest amusement.

"Well…" said Pomeroy. "We shall unpack our things and see you downstairs presently. With scones."

"With scones," she agreed. "And tea."

"At which time we shall have to subject you and your husband to further questioning." Laughter echoed from down in the kitchen, but the woman in their company smiled no more.

"My husband is not here."

"Oh." Flaxton consulted his watch. "What time does he usually return from work?"

"Flaxton."

"I'm afraid he will not return." The fingers of Mrs Willett's right hand touched the circumference of a wedding ring on her left. As she revolved it she chose not to meet the eyes of either man, instead moving to a jug and bowl on the dressing table next to a landscape in oils depicting a cow and a mill, in pale and rather insipid imitation of Constable. The light of the afternoon falling through the window she gazed out of did her a great service.

"Fergus was taken in the war whilst defending a bridge. The very last days. Like an insult. I have numerous letters. He wrote frequently, as I grew larger. Expectant in every way. Lizzy-May, bless her, was born only a few weeks after I received the news. He wanted a son, as all men do."

"I daresay he would have doted on her," said Flaxton before coughing lightly into his hand again. The country air had made his throat inescapably dry.

As if apologising for a sign of weakness, she said: "I can't help but be sad she will never know him."

Silence greeted that slight but devastating remark. Flaxton felt adrift. Words seemed shamefully inadequate, and even Pomeroy felt unable to conjure ones that were sufficient or appropriate.

"I looked after those poor officers," she said, "but I could not look after him." A twitch of her cheek told of her sense of the grotesque irony.

"It is better to have loved and lost than never to have loved at all." Pomeroy tried not to imbue the well-worn quote with the honeyed tone of a platitude. Clearly the last thing the young widow wanted was pity.

"Are you married, Professor Flaxton?"

"I am not."

"And you, Mr Pomeroy?"

"No."

"There is still time," she said.

2

THEY had first met at an SPR lecture in South Kensington on the subject of Gurney's *Phantoms of the Living*, but had been aware of each other's presence beforehand, as of a lingering ghost or offstage character waiting to enter. Their interests overlapped – and not just 'crisis apparitions' – this much was clear, but in spying Pomeroy in person for the first time over the customary tea and biscuits after the talk, Flaxton was struck that this lanky, long-chinned individual mixed easily and garrulously, whilst he himself wanted to run for the hills in even the most convivial social setting. It was as if he was regarding, with some fascination, but at a safe distance, a different species.

He did not consider himself either dry or miserable, or indeed solitary, if that was a negative, and knew his life was built on solid and firm ground. Much more solid than that of others less fortunate than himself. Indeed, in his rare introspective moments he considered himself a very lucky man. But if he were to be approached by Pomeroy, and suffer that chummy handshake, he thought he would very probably die.

His reaction, then, was one of astonishment when, several lectures later, Pomeroy asked him to look over a paper he'd written for the Journal of the SPR discussing mediumship in relation to light, electricity, and magnetism, and add his two-penneth, if it wasn't too much of a burden.

Flustered, Flaxton declined.

The man persisted.

Thereafter, having eventually supplied him with a few gratefully-received notes – pointing out, amongst other things, that zinc and silver produce a taste when in voltaic communication, not from galvanic concussion – Flaxton found himself invited over, by way of thanks, to see Pomeroy's library, pompously declared to consist of thousands of books on their shared topic, the shadow land where conventional science feared to tread. Flaxton caught the wrong bus, arriving hot and bothered, saying yes to a cup of tea but receiving something much more potent. The evening was then spent largely fighting to overcome his nerves. Pomeroy picked up a book at random and read from it. They sat opposite each other in warmth of a crackling fire, feet almost touching.

Pomeroy wore a silk smoking jacket. Flaxton a tweed suit that had seen better days. Pomeroy said he should spoil himself.

"Why, I've nobody to dress up for."

"One can dress up for one's self." Pomeroy crossed his long legs, naked feet in Persian slippers. Flaxton excused himself and caught the last bus home.

Once, alone in a café off The Strand after a book-buying expedition, he glimpsed Pomeroy passing. It was undoubtedly him. Thin, debonair. Pencil moustache. Homberg hat at a jaunty angle. Raincoat folded over one arm. Flaxton shrank away from the window, fearful to be spotted. Fearful of what, he did not know. Seclusion had always been a comfort. Seclusion and books. Equations and figures. Problems that could be worked out on paper, or with a slide rule, because mathematics was logical. Every action having an equal and opposite reaction.

Pomeroy asked him to accompany him on a trip to Ravenna for Christmas, with friends, to see the mosaics. Terrified at the prospect, Flaxton said he had a duty to spend the yuletide with his mother. Family obligations, though he had no family.

Why did anyone think he was the type who would relish plodding around a basilica getting sunstroke? And why did Pomeroy, of all people, pursue him so? The question was utterly perplexing. Did he see some quality in Flaxton that Flaxton failed to see in himself?

Feeling guilty, once spring came, he suggested to Pomeroy a trip to a castle in Wales. A faux-baroque chateau near Cardiff built by the Marquis of Bute, which looked as if it had been transplanted from the Rhine Valley. There had been stories of a treasure guarded by three spectral eagles. The weekend had proved uneventful but pleasant, Pomeroy's impatient strides leading the way up the hill. Muddy boots side by side outside a squat stone pub.

A few weeks later they acquired two seats at a concert of Edward German's *Merrie England* at the Albert Hall. Flaxton voiced his concern over the exorbitant price of the tickets. "You only live once, old boy," said his companion. Feeling the proximity of another man in the dark, shoulder touching shoulder, was extraordinary to Flaxton, the warmth of two adjacent bodies very different from the icy dungeon where they'd waited for the beat of ghostly wings and the snap of ghostly beaks. Flaxton eagerly joined in the applause at the curtain, as elated as if he had run a mile. "Bravo!" Pomeroy took to his feet. "Bravo!" Flaxton stood as well. His knees felt like jelly. They went off their separate ways home. One to Wembley, one to Muswell Hill.

It was an unlikely pairing, the Cambridge physicist and the self-educated nuts-and-bolts man.

"There's a haunted pub in Ipswich. I thought we might give it the once over."

On that occasion, it was Pomeroy who provided a reason to decline. "An invitation from friends." Flaxton took this as a rebuff. He was quietly devastated, but said it didn't matter.

Then followed a hiatus.

Flaxton half-expected to bump into him in one of their bibliophilic haunts off Charing Cross Road of a Saturday, but never did. He asked one book dealer who had come to know them, and their reading preferences, if he ever saw Pomeroy these days. Alone, or with someone else.

"A friend, you mean?"

"Yes, friend, or lady friend, or wife…"

"No, never with a wife, sir, no." The bookseller appeared to want to furnish Flaxton with information he did not request. "You know, he's not posh. Those airs and graces are all put on. He's nothing but an actor when all's said and done. Comes from a working class family who live in a terraced house in Stepney. His mother was a skivvy. He's nothing but a fake."

Placing coins down for a thin volume on *Ghosts and Goblins* by Charles Lamb, Flaxton felt he had to defend his associate. "If you ask me, he's entitled to live his life in any way he chooses. Good day."

At the next lecture at the Institute of Clairvoyance and Spiritual Science, Flaxton saw Pomeroy with another man his junior. He decided not to approach them but saw Pomeroy looking over at him a number of times as if to solicit a reaction. Flaxton went to dinner afterwards at his club in the company of Franc Dorling, Morris Pritchard and Reg Cottam. The Cambridge Telepathy crowd. Pomeroy's chair was empty. Flaxton had to endure the beastly Annapurna Lloyd droning on about cross correspondence experiments in Dorking.

So it was a surprise when Pomeroy contacted him out of the blue suggesting they team up for the current investigation. Flaxton agreed to do it, but was careful not to exhibit undue enthusiasm in the wording of his reply, though he did mail it by return of post.

3

THE evening meal provided was hearty but plain. A delicious, steaming shepherd's pie which Flaxton had no hesitation in praising as delicious as he mopped up the thick gravy with anticlockwise sweeps of crusty bread.

"The French do tend to overembellish."

"Mrs Ready can never be accused of that." Their demure host had not changed for dinner – which she called 'tea'– and still wore her gingham house dress. An informality Flaxton found charming.

Pomeroy had declared himself vegetarian, and insisted on no meat. He said gurus in the East swore by it. "Sharpens the mind. Improves the constitution." Flaxton thought it faddish. For afters they indulged in sliced peaches from a tin and evaporated milk.

Two notebooks were opened. Two fountain pens uncapped.

They asked of noises, knockings, unexplained happenings of any kind?

Mrs Willett shook her head. "Sometimes there is a trail of mud when Lizzy-May goes up the road with a basket of carrots to feed the ponies, but no, nothing." She told of how many times she had been forced from her bed – *thrown* was her expression. "It has become quite unstoppably violent. Once begun it does not abate, even with the most ardent prayers. The vicar came, from Sheppardine. He could do nothing."

"Did he sleep in it overnight?" asked Flaxton.

"He said he could not."

Her daughter had, unavoidably, heard the ructions too, and on a few occasions saw it 'in flagrante'. As a consequence, for several weeks now, Mrs Willett had been compelled to abandon her own room and share a bed with Lizzy-May in order to get a decent night's sleep.

"Have any guests used the room?" asked Flaxton.

"No. You are the first."

"You didn't feel the need to find out if others would experience the same thing?"

Holding his gaze, Mrs Willett repeated simply: "You are the first."

She had revealed enough information about herself for Flaxton to commit a pen portrait to his notebook, and not an unfavourable one. Her father, who had been dead some time, hailed from Easingwold. Her mother from Lille; hence she spoke English and French with equal capacity. Flaxton noted that she was physically fit and mentally more than capable, had no dependency on medication that might affect her sensory reliability, took wine with dinner, which appeared to be her greatest vice, and, even in these most trying of circumstances, conveyed a temperament which was, if not cheerful, pleasant. In short, of her probity and incapacity for deception he had every reason to be convinced.

"Mrs Ready saw a ghost once," piped up Lizzy-May, whose potato and mince had been separated on the plate from her green beans by a dictatorial fork. "One night she took a short cut home through the graveyard, when she heard a chink, chink, chink, and thought 'Whatever is that?' She parted the bushes and looked over and, under the pale, pale moonlight, saw a man kneeling at a gravestone with a hammer and chisel, chipping away. 'Whatever are you doing,' she said, 'out here in the dead of night?' The man looked round at her with round, baleful eyes and said: 'They spelt my name wrong.'"

Pomeroy almost lost his mouthful of peaches and evaporated milk. He pointed at her with his spoon. "Very good. Very good."

Flaxton laughed and dabbed each side of his mouth with his napkin – or what Mrs Willett called a 'serviette'.

"Time for bed, young lady," said Mrs Ready. "I'll tell her a story, then I'll be off."

"No more like that one, I trust."

The char lady rolled her eyes, neither confirming nor denying the comic tale had originated from her. "I've done two hot water bottles for the gentlemen."

"I doubt we shall need them."

"You will."

As soon as the cook and child were out of earshot, Pomeroy took a cigarette from his case.

"A force to be reckoned with."

"The firm hand my daughter needs. She takes no nonsense."

"The little one has a wise head on young shoulders."

The bowl of Flaxton's pipe glowed with the touch of a match. "Not backward in coming forward."

"Better than not speaking at all."

"I was brought up that children should be seen and not heard. And preferably not seen either."

"I can't bear having her out of my sight," Mrs Willett said, barely above the volume of a thought. She rose to clear the plates. Flaxton wondered why it was that maid and not mother took the child to bed. It only made him think again of that framed photograph of the army officer.

"The supernatural." The widow returned to the kitchen table with more composure, though it seemed the tobacco smoke irritated her eyes. "Is it all Anne Boleyn with her head under her arm? If so, I shall feel very inadequate."

"Oh no, we have phantom nuns and black monks galore," said Pomeroy. His act of smoking always had an almost balletic grace to it. "Powerful acts or emotions in the past sometimes leave an etheric trace. A residue. Think of it as a recording which a gramophone, of sorts, may play when the needle drops."

Flaxton had to admit Pomeroy talked a good talk, but wondered if the man's flummery amounted to anything truly scientific. He'd certainly be drummed out of the fastidiously disciplined university circle he himself moved in if he voiced such vague and unsupported conjecture. But Flaxton, in general, held back from branding the new, flamboyant breed of popular ghost hunters as 'thrill-seekers' who chased spooks for excitement and the odd book deal. He wouldn't stoop so low. Even if some of his colleagues did.

"Is that what you both think?"

Flaxton chewed his pipe stem. "We agree that such things occur which would seem to question the laws of physics."

"Other than that, we fight like cat and dog."

Flaxton greatly enjoyed the smile he saw widen on Mrs Willett's face, but it did not stay long before it withered.

At ten o'clock it the two gentlemen decided it was time to *levitate* to the bed chamber. Their host offered cups of Horlick's malted beverage to aid restful sleep. Pomeroy declined, pointing out they rather needed something to ensure they kept awake. Though no medical stimulant to disturb the senses. Perish the thought.

"Not even a dram of whisky? My husband swore by it."

"No. Thank you," said Flaxton. "It's imperative I maintain control of my senses."

"Oh, imperative." Pomeroy laughed. Flaxton wasn't sure if he should be offended by that, but the brisk slap on his arm made him dismiss such a worry as oversensitivity on his part.

"I hope the gulls on the roof won't disturb you in the morning."

"That's the least of our worries." Pomeroy took the woman's hand and kissed the back of it lightly.

Flaxton looked away. He fumbled with his pen and pocketbook, feeling his face glow yet again. Such familiarity was so beyond him the sight of it made him almost feel physically sick. He wished it didn't, but he knew it was the fabric of his being and something he could no more change than he could slough off his skin.

4

I say, Flaxton. Is it me, or did you feel a significant drop in temperature when you entered this room compared to the rest of the house?"

"The fire has been raging downstairs, old boy. Not surprising."

"Cold spot?"

"Possible."

"Unconvinced?"

"Until the evidence presents itself."

They heard a gentle knock on the door, followed by a woman's voice.

"We've used the bathroom. It's all yours."

"Thank you. Thank you so much."

Pomeroy took off his brown and white spectator shoes and placed them neatly under the vanity table. He unhooked his braces from his shoulders and began unbuttoning his trousers.

"I'll give you some privacy, then," said Flaxton.

"What? Oh. Yes. All right."

With his night clothes over his arm, Flaxton went down the landing and completed his ablutions. Towelling his face, he was sobered by the sight of the shaving accoutrements belonging to the late husband – Fergus, was it? There they stood, in front of him. Brush, razor, water cup, on the shelf above the sink, unused for ages but holding a talismanic value, like a holy relic in a small shrine. Flaxton could immediately see how impossibly hard it would be for the young widow to dispose of them. He put tooth powder on his brush. The water from the tap eventually chugged out and was icy on his gums.

In the mirror above the sink his moustache and eyebrows were grey. The hated jowls made him think of his father, whom he horribly resembled more with every passing day. *Tup-tup!* – Flaxton could remember him saying whenever, as a boy, he did something wrong or wasn't paying attention. *Tup-tup!*

Unable to look at his own visage for any great length of time, he stripped to his underwear and pulled on his night shirt and bed socks, which had been last dug out when he indulged in a hike on Mount Snowdon with twelve perfect strangers.

He returned to the master bedroom as Pomeroy left it, already dressed in his blue and white striped pyjamas, whistling the Radetsky March. They exchanged the candle holder. It gave a warm glow in contrast to that of the battery-powered flashlight rigged up in the corner, giving a spill of light up one wall. Flaxton was grateful for both. All the better to see you, he thought; whatever the *you* was, and whether it would be visible or not.

The two cameras leered at him and he leered back. The thermograph, the barometer, all in working order – yes, there to collect readings, there to collect proof. He climbed into one side of the bed – it had not been pre-arranged which – and he imagined Pomeroy would say he had chosen wrongly, just as his father would, in any given circumstance. Shivering, he tugged the blanket up to his chest. The heat of the hot water bottle had taken the majority of the chill off the sheets and slowly radiated up his body through his socks.

Pomeroy returned, opened his suitcase, took out a small blackboard and placed it on a cushion on the window seat, placing a stick of chalk from a packet on top. "If there is a spirit, it can make itself known."

Flaxton watched him sealing the windows and door edges with tape, writing his initials along the edges in order to detect tampering. Kneeling there on the floorboards like a religious supplicant at his devotions. Brushing the door handle with powdered graphite. "Potential fingerprints," he said, answering Flaxton's second unspoken question. "In case of chicanery."

"What do we do now?"

"We wait."

Pomeroy kicked off his slippers and slung himself under the covers. The springs protested with something akin to a groan. He punched the pillows. Writhed, then settled. The rough sea flattened. Flaxton was leafing through the book from the bedside table.

"Her reading material. *A Passage to India*. E. M. Forster."

"I'd have expected *Mrs Dalloway*."

Flaxton had not heard of it, but did not wish to advertise his ignorance. If Pomeroy had asked what he himself was reading – indeed, the book that was in his overnight bag, and which had been a good companion on his train journey – Flaxton would have said Oparin's *The Origin of Life*. But Pomeroy did not ask.

"Don't hog the bottle," Flaxton snapped. "You have your own."

"Sorry."

"Bottle hog."

"Sorry."

Footsteps to the bathroom. Light ones. Lizzy-May. They lowered their voices to whispers.

"Observations?"

"Several," said Flaxton.

"Of what kind?"

"Of the obvious kind, I think."

"The girl reported clearly that she heard the phenomenon – and saw it, to boot."

That cut no ice with Flaxton. "Do you not think the reported speech of her mother could assert itself in her mind so vividly as to be indistinguishable from truth, and be recounted as such, in the first person?"

"False reporting in the mind of a malleable child?"

"Quite. Your alternative?"

"I have none. Though she does not strike me as malleable."

"What does she strike you as?"

The water closet flushed as the chain was pulled. The two men listened to the padding of small feet.

"We shall see what we shall see," said Pomeroy. "Or hear."

"The proof is in the pudding."

"Indeed."

"Indeed."

"What time is it?"

Flaxton consulted the luminous hands of the travel clock at his elbow. "Getting on for midnight."

"Should we sleep, three hours on, three hours off? As in the trenches?"

"You nod off first."

"I don't believe I could."

"Four eyes open are better than two."

"Quite."

Mention of trenches brought it back to Flaxton. He'd been mobilized in 1915. Served on four different ships. Three had been sunk in the space of six months. Pomeroy had been medically rejected due to heart deficiency. He'd been desperate to get in the Royal Flying Corps but failed due to colour blindness. Ended up doing night shift in a factory making shell fuses. Said it reminded him of bodging around in his father's tool shed. The two men barely talked of the war, as men of that generation were wont. Flaxton had once said "If you've seen someone face down in the North Sea, you don't believe in some 'ether'. There is no ether. There is just this." Pomeroy had replied: "But what is the point if there is 'just this'?" Flaxton had said: "We can believe in fairyland or we can believe in the truth." Pomeroy's rejoinder was: "What if fairyland *is* the truth?"

Now he said: "What are you thinking?"

"Of a wife's loss," Flaxton said quietly. "And her pain every time she looks into her daughter's face and sees the vestige of her husband. Ghastly."

"But perhaps beautiful, in its way."

Flaxton attempted to make himself comfortable. "Would it be possible for a child to creep in, crawl under the bed whilst her mother slept, make it rise, bang and thrash, and get out of the room in the dark?"

Pomeroy chuckled. "Jolly japes."

"It's a theory. And not a fantastical one."

"No, if the child has the strength of four men. Come on, old bean."

The response hurt Flaxton. The dismissiveness. The feeling he was an idiot and would always be an idiot. He could almost hear his father again – *Tup-tup! Tup-tup!*

Pomeroy drained the glass of water he'd brought up with him.

"Good grief," said Flaxton. "My bladder would not thank me for that at 4 a.m."

"Ah! The medicinal properties of Adam's ale far outweigh the temporary inconvenience of the call of nature. A glass at night is good for the heart and kidneys. Fights muscle cramps and aids hydration. I've read a great deal on the subject."

"No doubt."

Pomeroy blew out the candle. They were not plunged into complete darkness. The battery of the torch would last well into morning.

"Sleep well, old chap."

"I shan't."

"Neither shall I. We have a job to do."

Flaxton picked up his box of Swan Vestas from the bedside table. The glare of the struck match touching the Revelation in his pipe lit up his face in the gloom.

"Loosen your scarf," said Pomeroy. "It's not the Arctic."

"It might be."

"I was thinking of your comfort."

"Well don't."

5

SO progressed the night in which nothing happened. Presently there echoed a tap, tap, tap, as the pipe tobacco was dislodged into an ashtray, followed shortly by the distinctive, circular scraping sound as it was cleaned with the blade of a pen knife. In the near-dark Pomeroy, unseen, or semi-unseen, cleared his throat. He had his knees raised and his notebook propped up on his thighs but was not writing and seldom moved, save for the irritating habit of removing then replacing the cap of his pen.

Flaxton's eyelids had become heavy. He periodically had to blink to keep them open. He could testify with scientific accuracy that, since the God-given – or Mrs Ready-given – hot water bottles had lost their lustre, his fingertips and nose were frozen to the point of numbness. The night temperature had fallen more dramatically than either of them had foreseen – or *he* had foreseen, anyway – though he didn't feel the need to attribute it to anything of the 'ether'.

At 2 a.m. Pomeroy had asked if he wanted another blanket. Flaxton had told him he was all right and not to fuss.

It was now an hour later, and silent, except for the unpredictable scratch-scratching of the mice in the wainscoting about which they'd been warned. Flaxton imagined the creatures nosey about the uninvited guests invading their territory, little pink feet scurrying from wall to wall, up, down, and across. It became, in his mind, diagrammatic. To him, all things became so, eventually. He made no apology for admitting – and had said so on many an occasion – if he could not reduce a thing to sums or geometry or algebra, he had difficulty believing the thing could exist at all.

He tugged off his scarf – which he feared might give him a heat rash – and let it dangle and drop to the floor beside the bed.

The world around him was chill, but he felt a soft heat emanating from the human body lying next to him. This was peculiar and unusual. He pondered when he last felt that. When last he shared a bed. It must have been his mother's bed when he was ill as a child and craved comfort. Tugging the blanket, not sure he would get a whack from his father. Wetting the bed. Oh, yes. That was the other thing. The thing that drove his father into a rage. Something his little body couldn't control. No more than his father could control his temper. He remembered the sight of his mother weeping gently as Father once beat him with his slipper for some misdemeanour he could not now remember. But he remembered her face and her pleading for mercy on his behalf. He remembered the dark. Yet had it been night, or day?

He was not asleep, and, no, not dreaming. Merely thinking.

His eyes fixed on the stained, dark beams above and the plasterwork between. The four-poster had a wooden frame around the top, but no canopy as such. He wondered why. He wanted his vision to become accustomed to the dark, but darkness did not lessen its grip, perhaps because of the way Pomeroy had sealed the cracks around the windows and door. No light could enter. No air. No goodness, he almost felt. The room took on the fustiness of cramped bunk beds and steel corridors below sea level. The unseemly reek of bodily functions that go with panic, dread and enforced intimacy.

Eyes open or eyes shut, it did not much matter, so Flaxton let them close to help rest his mind from such pointless wanderings.

A weight shifted next to him. He felt a lightness under him that shook him slightly and made him dizzy. *Levitation?* No. His companion had turned, or sat up. Flaxton could not tell which, but the mattress had soughed, its springs protesting. He felt the valley between them deepening. He would be sucked down into it if he didn't adjust his centre of gravity.

The bed – the *offending* bed – quickly settled, not abnormally.

He could hear no sound outside the house. No rain, no wind, no birds, no owl, no plaintive vixen. No traffic, as he was used to from his rooms in London, from the comfort of his home. There was no comfort here. This was a comfortless place. Why did he think that? Was he, in spite of his intellect, prey to the same associations and suggestions as those of a lower education, or none? It struck him as never before that in the dark – the *truly* dark – there was no student to impress, no blackboard to fill with chalk marks, it was as if the blackness itself stripped one to the barest feelings, a rabbit skinned and ready for the pot.

He leaned over to consult the luminous hands of the clock.

It read 3.37.

He committed this to memory for no other reason than he did, and counted the seconds from one to a hundred, then a hundred more, backwards, from ninety-nine to zero. Numbers. Numbers. Numbers…

Pomeroy did not snore. Nor did he, apparently, breathe.

Flaxton concentrated hard without moving a muscle, but no – nothing, nothing *audible* emanated from the lump under the blanket next to him. So much so that Flaxton began to wonder if Pomeroy was alive at all.

Which was preposterous. Yet as seconds ticked by his sense of panic deepened. His heart beat faster. Part of his autonomous nervous system and so beyond his conscious control.

"Pomeroy?" he said to the room, not daring, nor wishing, to open his eyes.

The mattress soughed once more. This time not just registering a weight shifting, but one shifting *closer*, then settling again – heavily. His arm flat under the blanket, he found himself gripping the bed sheet tightly with one clawed hand, the other, nearer the centre of the bed, tucking icily behind his lower back. His coccyx.

A second later he felt something placed on his chest, the innate warmth spreading from it through his cold, prone body. The warm thing lifted then touched the side of his throat, near the jugular, then his cheek.

Flaxton could not move.

Some voice in his mind said: *"There is nothing to be afraid of. Nothing. Why are you so afraid?"*

The warmth then that he knew was a hand returned to nestle upon his sternum. And his father's voice, as if coming from a badly-tuned wireless, said *You fool, who would want you? Who would want you?*

He felt breath, breath from another – intangible, invisible. He could smell Pomeroy's cigarettes so very strongly and powerfully.

His own breath refused to leave his body. Something twisting within his chest escaped in a sound that was not even a word, not even a syllable. A cry for help. Inaudible but to himself.

He shot up to a seated position on the side of the bed, gripping the mattress, gasping and light-headed. His stockinged feet felt the security of the floor. He felt a touch – a *touch* – on the bare flesh between the collar of his night shirt and the side of his neck, under the ear, just below where he shaved. He did not let it grip him. It slid off his skin instantly as he stood erect.

The Professor's fumbling fingers wrestled with the door handle, leaving his smudged marks in the graphite powder. He let out a sob of gratitude when it turned. He did not look back. As he yanked open the door, all the seals around it – ponderously autographed by Pomeroy's initials – broke, ripping away with a sticky shriek as if peeled off a wound. He stumbled out onto the dark of the landing, the draught created by his hasty exit causing the small hemispheres of the Robinson anemometer to spin agitatedly.

The door was ajar, and he left it so. The tiny squeaks of the metal hemispheres accompanying him as he fled.

6

"NOTHING happened." These were Professor Flaxton's words, firmly spoken, as he sat hunched in the porter's chair near the door to the living room, wrapped in the striped mustard and oatmeal throw he had dragged from the bed in the haunted room, which he now wore as a shawl around his shoulders. "We saw nothing. We heard nothing. There *was* nothing."

Mrs Willett, wrapped in a dressing gown, regarded his thick woolly socks and the white skin of his shins before clutching the collar of her night dress to her throat and looking crestfallen. The low sun of dawn had awakened in the East and shone through a strategically placed stained-glass window at the back of the hall, a remnant of the house's ecclesiastical past.

"I'm sorry," she said weakly and defensively, moving out of its illumination, not meeting his eyes, and hurrying into the kitchen, where she put on a kettle of water to boil.

Pomeroy appeared on the staircase, heralded by the creaking of his footfalls on the steps as he descended,

87

fully dressed, and more than usually immaculate, freshly shaven, with his hands in his pockets.

"Old boy."

"Nothing happened," Flaxton repeated – for his benefit.

"Do you think I'm a liar?" asked the widow.

"Not at all," said Pomeroy.

"Things can be imagined to be true." Flaxton lifted himself to his feet, tying the throw around his waist in rather the manner of a kilt, and spoke gently. "It doesn't mean they, they objectively happened, in reality, according to, to, to—" He stammered. "Well, according to *scientific principles*, you see."

Pomeroy walked past the Professor into the kitchen. "It did not buck. There was no bucking."

Flaxton could not be clear whether Pomeroy was addressing him or the lady of the house, as his gaze appeared to fix upon neither.

"I know what I felt," insisted Mrs Willett. "On several occasions. On numerous occasions."

"Of course, my dear. We do not doubt your testimony. But, as my friend, the esteemed physicist, says, he cannot falsify his own experience."

Flaxton addressed Pomeroy. "And you?"

Now that Pomeroy turned to face him, Flaxton perceived, he was sure he perceived, the flicker of a smile. "The same. A coldness registered on the thermograph. Also a disruption when you left the room, leaving your fingerprints on the door handle."

Flaxton looked at the dark stains of graphite on his fingers.

"I'm sorry, old man."

"Nothing unusual or abnormal."

"Cold," repeated Flaxton. "That's the ticket. There we have it. That's all? For my report. To the Society."

"That is all."

"I must write it up on my return to London."

"You must."

The kettle whistled for attention. Mrs Willett warmed an inexpensive brown tea pot with a splash and a swirl.

"Bevis Adnams." Pomeroy's grin advertised his notably crooked teeth as he sat and crossed his legs. "The editor. Of the Journal. Frightfully nice chap. Penchant for darts." Flaxton puzzled over why that was even vaguely relevant and concluded it was not.

"I can't help but be crushingly disappointed." Mrs Willett dolefully placed cups and saucers in front of her two guests. "You came all this way, and…"

"Mama!" Lizzy-May fluttered downstairs, giving her teddy a ride down the banister rail in the process. "Fluffy Tonks says he slept all the way through the night without any bad dreams!"

"I'm very glad to hear it," said Pomeroy.

"You trust me to get it right?" asked Flaxton.

"Always."

Slapping his knees, Pomeroy leapt up, grabbing Lizzy-May by the hand, rather unexpectedly for Lizzy-May. He dashed to fetch his coat from its peg.

"Come along, young lady! We shall walk to the churchyard and back before the Professor and I catch our taxi to the station. I told the driver to return at noon." The little girl brokered no objection to this plan, in fact was more than delighted at the prospect, as soon as she had received the approval of her mother's expression, and wasted no time in donning her apricot long sleeve, capelet, beret, and scarf.

"By the time you get back I'll have tea and toast on the table."

Lizzy-May slipped her feet into Wellington boots. "I'll show you Mr Warren's skewbald!"

"Well, what a treat that will be. You know, we don't have horses in London," Pomeroy teased as the girl ran out into the garden, letting in the twittering of birds eager for the early worm.

"Mr Pomeroy? Can I ask you one more thing?"

Flaxton was slightly aggrieved that the woman addressed her question to his colleague, when he himself sat across the table from her.

"You are the expert in these matters. Tell me honestly, please. Will I be able to use the master bedroom again? Will my life ever return to normal?"

Pomeroy glanced at Flaxton. Flaxton thought it was up to him how he answered.

"I wholly expect it shall, Mrs Willett, if you let it. Your husband would not blame you if you were to move on. From the house, or from the bed. A new start. A new life. I do not believe in many certainties, but I believe in one. We must live because they do not."

As Pomeroy closed the front door after him, Flaxton fetched the sugar bowl, ashamed and perplexed that such a sentiment could be – and had been – voiced by his ill-educated colleague and not by him. He remembered his father, the bank manager, once calling emotional intercourse 'cake decorations' – of no use to the serious, material progress of life, and felt a cloud of sadness pass over him that it had not occurred to him, but had occurred to Pomeroy, to offer the young widow some kind of solace.

She stood at the sink with her back to him. He heard gentle sniffles she attempted to keep silent, extracting a telltale handkerchief from the cuff of one sleeve.

"She will be fine." Flaxton spoke hesitantly, imagining – perhaps wrongly – she was concerned for her daughter's future without a father. "She's an intelligent girl. Shower her with praises occasionally."

"I shall."

In life, any display of distress upset Flaxton immensely and he could not bear its proximity, but he did not think it an unconscionably selfish act to absent himself by retreating upstairs to get dressed.

He peeled the wretched sticky tape from around the door, scrunched it into a ball and tossed it into the waste paper basket next to the cold, now-redundant hot water bottles. The morning sun did not cast its benevolence on this side of the building, evidently, because the bedroom was no less frozen than it had been the previous night. His colleague's 'ghost-seeking' equipment was not yet packed. The room was a mess. Flaxton lifted the thermograph, the travel clock, and Pomeroy's notebook onto the vanity table. In the mirrors he could not avoid the multiple reflection of the mountain ranges and river beds of the disrupted bedsheets behind him. Keen to let in fresh air, he moved one of the camera tripods to one side, peeled away more of the dashed sealing tape, and opened the casement window.

At the far end of the garden he spied Lizzy-May skipping towards the tumulus, where a winding path led through a wrought iron gate to a graveyard of loppy tombstones. Pomeroy followed at a leisurely pace, waving hello to Mrs Ready as she arrived on her bicycle, its bell tinkling cheerily. Suddenly overcome with an unaccountable weariness, Flaxton lay for a few minutes on the bed, stretched out flat, while the voices of man and child grew faint.

He sat up quickly, the blood rushing to his head producing a moment of dizziness, then stood, bundling the dirty sheets into a pile and leaving them on the floor, as he'd been instructed. Mrs Ready would take care of the laundry when they had left. All would be in order.

He washed and shaved in the bathroom, grateful for the cold water on his face. He felt heady, as if he'd been out in the sun, which was absurd. Returning to the bedroom, he dressed, packed his overnight bag and zipped it up.

On the floor he saw the small blackboard Pomeroy had left out with a stick of chalk resting on top of it, in case a message came from the spirit world. He walked over to it and picked it up. Nothing had been written. The board was blank.

7

PROFESSOR Flaxton attended no more of the monthly lectures announced by the SPR. He had simply become less enamoured with the idea of a trek across London, and found that he could attain all the information he required on up-to-date developments in the field of psychical research from editions of the Journal and Proceedings, sent to him as part of his membership, in a form he could peruse and absorb at his leisure, between commitments at King's College. Henceforth teaching, reading, and writing quite happily – *very* happily – would account for the majority of his time. He bought a single ticket and attended, alone, a concert of the Croydon Philharmonic Society's performance of Elgar's *Dream of Gerontius*, but found the behaviour of the audience bordering on the unruly, which not only inhibited his enjoyment but made him realise he had incubated for some time an increasing anxiety regarding social intercourse. He vowed thereafter to keep his own company and limit his private pleasures to the pursuit of subjects that interested and absorbed him. So when the Society asked him to engage in a further investigation, his first impulse was to refuse. He said he was too busy. He was sure *Pomeroy* would do it. But Pomeroy, he was told, had already said no, as he was off to explore occult rituals on the site of the witch trials of Würzburg. In the end, Flaxton couldn't help but succumb to the flattery of the editor and consequently found himself despatched off to endure the rigours of the English countryside; specifically Stanton Drew in Somerset, which possessed a stone circle that legend claimed to be petrified wedding guests known as 'The Devil's Dancers'. It was said, charmingly, that whoever tried to count the stones would drop dead before they finished the task. The catalyst for Flaxton's visit, however, was the apparition, it was alleged, of a small girl knocked down by an inopportune carriage outside the boarding house in which he now sat, where the breakfasts were reliable, the landlady gratifyingly mute, and the location agreeable.

Sunlight greeted the day but the sky was undecidedly ordinary outside the bay window. To the pleasing, if sonorous, tick-tock of a grandfather clock, he decapitated his egg to reveal a runny yolk done to perfection.

He habitually brought a book down to breakfast – it provided a necessary barrier to the possibility of idle conversation – but was horrified to find he had left his copy of the new edition of *Principia Mathematica* by A. N. Whitehead and Bertrand Russell in his room. He had been looking forward to plunging into deep theories, his excitement at the prospect exceeding even his enjoyment of the ovoid in front of him, but it was not to be.

Left with little alternative, he walked over to the small table by the fireplace and availed himself of the *Daily Mirror*. Not a periodical he would normally patronise, but the copy of *The Times* provided by the owners of the establishment had already been snatched by an owlish, rotund man who sat beside a curly-haired lad of sixteen or seventeen. Flaxton had previously noticed them the night before when he'd observed the owl instructing the youth how to properly eat his soup. The boy had furrowed his brow as if the task was beyond him and on one occasion caught Flaxton's eye from under his shaggy fringe before Flaxton lowered his gaze to his own Brown Windsor. There was no sign of a wife, but that meant nothing.

The front page told of a new Socialist MP for West Ham, the latest serial film starring an American boxer, and activities in Soviet Russia. Not until page five was he brought up short, his newly-poured tea cup placed carefully back on its saucer.

The photograph was grainy. The bulbous carving of one of the struts of the four-poster bisecting the foreground. Beyond, two men sat propped up against pillows like dummies; he more like a dummy than most, with his preposterous expression. Ghastly moustache. Bulbous cheeks of a grinning clown. And Pomeroy – almost dignified by comparison. The camel coat with velvet collar. Long chin. Small lips embellished with the pencil moustache.

The headline, which caused his eyebrow to tilt, read:

A GLOUCESTER 'POLTERGEIST'

He noticed immediately the names of the participants (excepting their own) had been changed, to protect anonymity – as he'd have expected. Pomeroy at least had the integrity to do that, even if, appallingly, his first port of call to publish his version of their investigation was a Fleet Street rag. Flaxton tried not to bridle. Pomeroy's dalliances with the popular press were his stock in trade; he made no secret of it.

The journalist's literary style was accomplished, if stodgy, and the situation described accurately – if, on occasion, it veered into little more than an interview. Flaxton had a curiosity about the contents, but no *great* curiosity. His own account in the Journal of the SPR, he was confident, would be seen as the *definitive* source. He absorbed it, then, as he sipped his tea, without any vast expectation of illumination.

> *"There is a theory, a theory gathering traction in some quarters, regarding the poltergeist or noisy spirit of the Germans. Some say it is a phenomenon – that is to say knocking, banging, and general disruption centred around, or caused by, a young girl going through the changes of pubescence. Such changes creating a psychic energy of pent-up violence which has nowhere to go but exact itself on ordinarily inanimate objects."*

Flaxton emitted a sigh.

"But rest assured," Pomeroy said, "when the child grows, she will grow out of it. I am convinced. I've been told the girl in question will start a new school in September. I have no difficulty predicting that once she leaves the house, the spirit tantrums will cease."

The thought of the little girl he had recently met at Oldbury-on-Severn, trailing her beloved teddy down the banister rail, soon swooning over boys filled Flaxton with a sense of unaccountable sadness.

He read on, to the end. He did not know why. He had been there. He knew perfectly well what had happened and what had not. As Pomeroy confirmed, in his way.

"The bed did not move," the Ghost-Seeker said from behind a wistful smile. "Sadly. Very sadly for Professor Flaxton and myself. Whatever it was, it didn't want to come out and play that night."

Flaxton grunted.

He had to have a grudging admiration for the man's audacity. Shaking his head as well as the newspaper, he refused to let it annoy him. Pomeroy's career as a scientist or showman was, after all, none of his business. What he said to the great British public was his own affair.

"I am a great advocate of the idea that life is a journey, not a destination. As a great philosopher once said, most human beings believe that the day their mother gives birth to them, that's it, the job is done, whereas in fact you have to spend your whole life giving birth to yourself."

Further down the page Pomeroy's face was framed by the columns of newsprint. The well-known photograph of him standing in his Laboratory of Psychic Education amongst test tubes and galvanometers, in shirtsleeves and braces with his hands on his hips. The working man, seeking spirits in his nuts and bolts.

Flaxton looked up again at the photograph of the two of them propped up in that four poster bed in their suits and waistcoats. The thin faced one at ease with the camera, and life. The startled-looking one with the thick moustache, the face of a fool. A person unable to be loved.

He stared at the egg on his spoon for a moment, then placed it at the side of his plate.

He folded the *Daily Mirror* in half, walked over and dropped it onto the pile of old newspapers next to the grate, ready to be used by the landlady to set the next day's fire.

Stephen Volk created BBCTV's notorious "Halloween hoax" *Ghostwatch* and the ITV paranormal drama series *Afterlife*. His many other screenplays include *The Awakening* (2011) starring Rebecca Hall and Gothic starring Natasha Richardson as Mary Shelley. He is a two-time British Fantasy Award winner, and the author of four collections: *Dark Corners*, *Monsters in the Heart*, *The Parts We Play* and *Lies of Tenderness*. His acclaimed *Dark Masters Trilogy* features the characters of Peter Cushing, Alfred Hitchcock and Dennis Wheatley respectively, while *Under a Raven's Wing* sees Sherlock Holmes and Poe's detective Dupin investigating bizarre crimes in 1870s Paris. His most recent book is *The Good Unknown and Other Ghost Stories* from Tartarus Press.

www.stephenvolk.net

Alight at top for
NETHERWOOD
EAST HILL LIFT, HASTINGS

Further Writings by the Same Author

DARK CORNERS
(Grey Friar Press, 2006)

MONSTERS IN THE HEART
(Grey Friar Press, 2013)

THE PARTS WE PLAY
(PS Publishing, 2016)

THE LITTLE GIFT
(PS Publishing, 2017)

THE DARK MASTERS TRILOGY
(PS Publishing, 2018)

COFFINMAKER'S BLUES:
COLLECTED WRITINGS ON TERROR
(Electric Dreamhouse, 2019)

UNDER A RAVEN'S WING
(PS Publishing, 2021)

LIES OF TENDERNESS
(PS Publishing, 2022)

THE GOOD UNKNOWN
AND OTHER GHOST STORIES
(Tartarus Press, 2023)

THE
DARK
MASTERS
TRILOGY
STEPHEN
VOLK

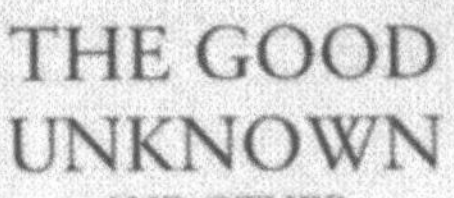

THE
PARTS
WE PLAY
STEPHEN
VOLK

LIES
OF STEPHEN VOLK
TENDERNESS

THE GOOD
UNKNOWN
AND OTHER
GHOST STORIES

Stephen Volk

Tartarus Press

How about
a DATE?

with a
GOOD BOOK

PoppyHarp
Simon Avery

CHEER THE SICK
VERITY
OLLOWAY

GREAT ROBOTS OF HISTORY
STORIES BY
TIM MAJOR

GREAT BRITISH HORROR 10
Something Peculiar
m
y Adams
lly Blades
rah Brooks
nma J Gibbon
mothy J Jarvis
hn Langan
m Major
exander Milner
rk Morris
nie Ware
rian Womack
edited by Steve J Shaw

GOOD BOOKS
WILL SATISFY
YOUR
CURIOSITY TOO!
READ MORE --
KNOW MORE

9 781917 173094